CITY OF ANGELS

/ / / /

CHANEL SMITH

MEDIUM MYSTERIES

Echo Park
Silver Lake
Hollywood Hills
City of Angels

Published by
Crop Circle Books
212 Third Crater, Moon

Copyright © 2016 by J.R. Rain & Chanel Smith

All rights reserved.

Printed in the United States of America.

ISBN- 9781687557261

Chapter One

Waking up with Mack had been a lot different from "waking up" with Mack. I'd been waking up with him for years, but not "waking up" with him. It took me a couple of seconds to decide how I felt about it, even before I opened my eyes and saw Mack's ghostly face staring at me from the other side of the bed.

"Good mahning, beautiful," he said, his thick Boston accent ever present. "How'd you sleep?"

"Not too bad," I smiled. Actually, it had been the best night's sleep I'd had in a while, though it had been well after midnight before the two of us had satisfied the built up tension that had been hovering around us for a good while. I was a little disappointed that he was back in his ghostly form, but I understood.

"It ought to have been good, because it's 11:30 in the mahning," he laughed.

I hadn't remembered sleeping that late since I was a teenager or whenever I happened to have hit the booze so hard that I was still passed out until midday. Feeling the sudden charge of guilt, I started to scramble out of the bed.

"Where're you going?" he asked. "It's Saturday. Isn't that your day off?"

I knew he'd read my mind and had heard the guilt go through my thoughts. It was Saturday and it was my day off, but I was an adult and… well, I needed to use the bathroom too.

He laughed as he read that thought. "I understand. One of the great benefits to being a ghost."

As I scrambled away to the bathroom, Mack was reclining against the pillow on the bed, actually, hovering slightly above it, with his fingers laced behind his head and a broad grin on his face.

I did my morning business and then looked at myself in the mirror. There was a new glow to my face, some might have called it the "well laid" look. It was solid evidence of a chain of events that had seemed like a dream. Mack really had become flesh, damned fine flesh, and we really had made love into the wee hours of the morning. I had been real. There was another part of my body, which hadn't seen action in a while, that was reminding me that it had been real as well.

"What are you doing in there, dahling?" I heard Mack calling out.

The bathroom, other than when he'd awakened me from sleeping in my own vomit a couple of weeks before, was the one room in the house where Mack wouldn't follow me. Was it really only a couple of weeks? It had seemed like a lifetime. So many changes had taken place; so many good changes. I smiled at myself in the mirror, something that I hadn't been in a habit of doing for a very long time. "You're going to be alright, Pauline," I told reflected image.

"What are you talking about in there?" Mack called at the door. I loved how his 'theres' sounded more like 'theahs.'

A wicked grin came to my face. I grasped the doorknob, turned it quickly, pulled the door open and said, "Nothing!"

"Were you trying to scare me, Pauline?" Mack asked.

"I guess not." Trying to scare a ghost was sort of a silly idea. I started laughing, which was something else I hadn't been doing a lot of lately, but I couldn't help myself. Something had been reborn in me; something childlike. I liked it.

"I like it too," Mack commented, having read my thoughts.

"I suppose that if we're going to be together, we really can't keep secrets anymore, right?" It was a rhetorical question, mostly meant for him, but I had an ulterior motive behind it.

"I suppose not," he answered, having read that part of my thoughts, but not expecting the next part.

"Can I ask you just one favor?"

"Of course," he answered.

"Can I still have the bathroom?"

The bathroom had been the one place where Mack had respected my privacy and allowed me to escape his mind reading. I had gotten used to having him read my thoughts, which wasn't all bad, but there were times—even when a woman was in love—that she needed her own place to escape to.

"You can have the whole house," he replied. "You only have to tell me when you need your space."

It was a major concession, one that I hadn't expected. "You're turning out to be quite tolerable."

"I could go back to turning over the chair," he teased.

"I like you this way," I said, extending my lips up for a ghostly peck, before heading to the kitchen.

I might have given up booze and cigarettes, but I wasn't going to give up coffee. I put together the fixings in the pot and waited for it to brew, while I looked out the kitchen window. Things had changed a lot. My last case with Amanda, in which I had almost died, had rattled me quite a bit, but it had rattled me in a good way, probably better than anything they might have been able to do in that high-dollar rehab clinic within the same amount of time.

It was funny how things worked out sometimes. I'd gone for a weekend "dry out" and ended up with a new friend, a case and an experience that scared me straight. I'd not only been scared straight, but my eyes had been opened into a whole new world of possibilities. That whole new world included Mack and me, which didn't sound half bad, and made that heart of mine expand 3 sizes… or was it 30 sizes? I laughed at the fact that I was trying to remember such a trivial thing from the Grinch. His dog's name was Mack, wasn't it?

"No, it was Max," Mack said, breaking into my conversation and giving me a start. He laughed as he saw me jump. "Now that's the way you do it."

Some things never changed. The coffee pot had finished gurgling and the thought of cartoons reminded me of the morning paper. It wasn't the Sunday edition with the big cartoon section, but it had the short black and whites. I hadn't read those in years.

"Hey, Mack, can you get the paper?"

"You mean that papah?" he asked, waving a shimmering hand toward the paper spread out on the table and open to the sports section.

"That would be the papah," I replied, trying to mimic his accent... and doing a horrible job. I filled my favorite mug with coffee from the pot and absently reached up and opened the cupboard where I'd kept my Captain Morgan. The moment that I did it, I realized that there were other things that hadn't changed. It was a stark reminder that I still had a battle to wage.

"You'll beat it, dahling," Mack whispered, smiling at me with a proud look.

"I hope so," I sighed. "I really don't want to go back."

Chapter Two

I'd separated the sports section and left it where Mack had been reading it and slid the section that had the cartoons and obits to the other side of the table where I could sip my coffee and have a few chuckles... over the cartoons, not the obits. I'd gotten up, flipped the paper closed and started to go refilled my cup, when a headline drew my attention, *Unexplained "Haunting" Events at Cal State Long Beach*. I was just about to dive into the story when there were three short knocks on my door. I froze. I knew that knock, but it was very unexpected. I looked toward Mack, who was beaming. He knew the knock too.

"Did you arrange this?" I asked, mocking his Bostonian accent.

"I am completely innocent," he replied.

"You'll never be completely innocent," I quipped. I considered my robe. It would be better if I put some clothes on. "Could you go ans—"

Mack was already on his way to the door before I finished the question. That was another of the perks involved in having a mind reading ghost living in your house.

While I was getting dressed, I recognized Julie's voice conversing with Mack from the front room. I could hear a third, trembling, male voice as well and wondered who might have come along with my unexpected visitor.

Though Julie had been a regular visitor and my best friend, my actions had pushed her away and gouged an enormous hole in our relationship. In fact, less than 24 hours before, I was pretty certain that our friendship might have been damaged beyond repair. Something had come up or she wouldn't have come to my house. I hurried to get dressed, sensing something very strange in the air. I checked myself in the mirror, sighed heavily, smiled at myself and started toward the front room.

"This is very unexpected," I began with a musical tone before I had rounded the corner into the front room. I wasn't prepared for what I saw.

Sitting in the overstuffed chair that Mack had previously enjoyed turning over in order to get my attention, was none other than... "Ford Mortimer?" I said the name aloud.

The guest that Julie had brought along with her had already been uncomfortable, but his eyes widened as I called out his name.

"Who's Ford Mortimer?" Julie wrinkled her brow, looked at her guest and then back at me.

"Or would you rather that I call you Blue?" I filled in with a smile on my face.

"How did you know my name?" he said in a quiet tone. His expression changed from a startled one to one of suspicion.

"Yes, do tell," Julie broke in.

"We've already met," I said and then gave him a couple of prompts. "Briar Summit Detox? Hollywood Hills? I was there for the rattlesnake roundup."

Blue paled as I made the last comment.

"I ah..." he started. "Yeah, that was ah..."

"I tried to warn you," I broke in, narrowing my eyes at him. Blue was an "authentic" shaman who performed a drumming ceremony at the spa/detox center that I'd attended the weekend before. I could tell that he had absolutely no idea what he was doing and playing with forces that he knew nothing about when he did his drumming ceremony. I had been right.

He'd called up a lot of dead natives who were extremely put out with what he was doing. In reaction to what he had done, they'd tossed a mess of rattlesnakes into the midst of the spa-goers and broken up the rest of the weekend. It had also created a rather difficult situation for me and my late, new friend, Amanda.

"Ten?" Recognition finally came to him. I'd been given the number ten to replace my name and maintain anonymity while I was at the detox center.

"I'd prefer being called Pauline," I responded.

I turned to look at Mack, who was grinning so broadly that it had to be hurting his face. I read his thoughts, which were mostly laughter at the expression on Blue's face. *This is hilarious!*

What's going on, Pauline? Julie's thoughts suddenly burst into my head.

"Okay, stop!" I said, looking in Mack's direction. "Please, Mack, help me out here. I'm trying to have a conversation."

I turned to Julie and smiled. "I'm proud of you, Jules; you've gotten good at that. I caught it, but it's really hard to concentrate on a conversation when there are two other voices talking to me, okay?"

"Who were you talking to?" Blue asked, his

blue eyes as wide as I'd ever seen anyone's eyes before. He was looking in Mack's direction and motioning with his hand before turning back to Julie. "Who was she talking to? What's going on?"

Julie opened her mouth to begin an explanation, but I stopped her.

"I've got this, Jules." I wasn't sure if I should be using my nickname for her since we were, technically speaking, on a friend break, but it was an old habit.

I looked directly at Blue. I tried to form the right words to explain who I was talking to and what was going on. I knew that Ford/Blue was a complete fake and there was a good bit of anger in me as I considered the mess that he had gotten Amanda, Mack and me into because of his carelessness. I was ready to unload on him, but I heard a voice in my head, Mack's voice, saying, *be nice.*

"Look, Blue," I began with a heavy sigh. "I am a real medium and a real psychic. I deal with real spirits. I was talking to my friend and live-in spirit, Mack."

I waved a hand in Mack's direction. As I did, I realized that "friend and live in spirit" was wholly inadequate to describe who and what Mack was to me and I felt a tingle of guilt about it.

It's okay; it isn't something he would understand anyway. We know who and what we are and that's all that matters.

With that little bit of encouragement from Mack, I smiled and pressed forward. A wicked thought came into my mind in the very same moment. I wasn't sure if it was my own or Mack's.

"He can reveal himself to you if you like?" I asked.

"No! No, that's okay," Blue waved his hands back and forth across each other in front of himself.

"Look, Blue," I started again. "You are probably an okay guy and simply have no idea what you're doing, but I have to be honest with you. You put myself and my friends into one hell of a tough situation because of that stunt you pulled at Briar Summit and I'm still pretty angry at you over it. I'm not sure why you're here, but I may not be the best person for you to consult with right now."

"Pauline!" Julie objected. She was newly miffed at me, though the last word from her was that she hadn't finished with being mad at me from before. "You haven't even heard what's going on yet? I brought him to you because there is a major problem that only YOU can fix."

"I appreciate your confidence in me," I responded, smiling at her. "But you, of all people, ought to understand where I'm coming from."

CHANEL SMITH

Chapter Three

"Would you at least listen, Pauline?" Julie whined.

I hadn't missed that particular part of our friendship. *The new Pauline, with the renewed heart, would at least listen.* I wasn't sure if the voice in my head was my own or Mack's, but I turned to look at him. He nodded and motioned for me to listen.

"Okay," I sighed. "I'll listen, but that doesn't guarantee anything."

I focused my attention on Blue and opened myself up to listen to him. For a medium, that means doing a lot more than just hearing the words that come out of a person's mouth. The instant I opened up to him, the headline from the paper flashed into my mind. I pushed it aside, but it popped up again. I tried to push it aside a second time, but it still wouldn't stay away.

"I think I screwed up even bigger," Blue started.

"What did you do at Cal State?" I asked. The vision of the article was associated with him for a reason. My intuition was already telling me what it was.

"You read the paper?" he asked.

"Actually, no, but I know whatever you're about to tell me has to do with something you did at Cal State, Long Beach, so go on."

"Well, the Native American Club at Cal State, L.B. invited me to come do a drumming for them…" he started.

"Oh no, you didn't, Blue," I broke in with an exasperated tone in my voice. "Didn't you learn anything at Briar Summit?"

"The gig had been booked weeks ago, before what happened at Briar Summit. I went to do it anyway. I didn't think anything bad would happen. I'm a shaman, I do drumming. People pay me to do this stuff. I mean, what am I supposed to do?"

"You're not a shaman," I responded. I tried to take the sting out of my next statement as best I could, but I knew it wasn't going to be easy. "You're a fraud, a charlatan, a wannabe, and you need to stop doing what you're doing before someone gets hurt."

"Pauline!" Julie objected.

"It's the truth and it has to be said. If you continue what you're doing, someone is going to get hurt or even killed."

"I'm afraid it's too late for that," he responded, lowering his eyes to the floor in front of him.

"Someone's already been killed?" I asked.

"No," he replied. "Just hurt, they'll pull through, but it was very bad."

"That's twice, Blue," I pointed out. I was trying to keep my anger under control, but it wasn't easy. "Have you learned anything yet?"

"I guess not," he muttered.

Watching him, hearing the tick, tick, tick of the clock and hearing Mack's soothing tone had me at a simmer. *Why are you so angry?* I knew that was my own question. It was easy enough to answer. I was angry because Blue had been toying with powers that he did not understand. He had disturbed spirits that hadn't wanted to be disturbed and he had unleashed a force that had the power to maim and destroy a lot of innocent people. *But he didn't know what he was doing.* I think that one was Mack's and he was right, as usual.

I shook my head and considered how much I

could use a smoke and a drink. *Pauline?* Mack's voice broke in. He didn't say anything else, but he brought the direction that my thoughts had started to take to my attention.

"The answer is no," I said, getting up from the couch and going into the kitchen in search of the mug and coffee that I had intended to drink before we were interrupted.

Julie started to get up and follow me. I held up a hand to stop her. "Not now," I said. "Just give me a minute."

I stopped Julie from following me, but I neither could nor wanted to stop Mack, though I made an attempt to ignore him as I went directly to the coffee pot, filled the mug, started to reach for the cupboard door and then turned away, leaning against the counter while I took a sip of the hot brew.

"You know what you ought to do," Mack said in a soft voice.

"Give me a second, Mack. I really don't want you to pressure me about this right now."

"I'm not pressuring you," he replied. "I was just going to tell you that maybe you should buy some of those syrups or coffee creamers that you can pour in your coffee. You know, just so you can continue the action without the consequence."

It wasn't a half bad idea. I'd had some of

those flavors in my coffee at Starbucks.

"Of course it is a good idea. I'm full of them."

"You're full of something," I teased. I was already starting to relax more. I decided to read the article that I'd seen earlier.

Pandemonium broke out resulting in two critical injuries and more than a dozen minor ones after a pow wow, sponsored by the Native American Students Association at the Long Beach campus of Cal State University, suddenly turned ugly. Student participants reported to have seen ghostly forms of ravens, bears, cougars and rattlesnakes attacking the circle where they were carrying out a drumming ceremony. "The drumming" said the shaman, referred to only as Blue, "is an ancient ritual that draws power from the spirits and allows participants to get in touch with their deeper selves."

It seems evident that many of the participants didn't get in touch with their deeper selves, but were, instead, terrified by the images that some of them claimed to have seen.

"It just came up at me on its hind feet and roared," said one of the students. "I wasn't sticking around. I don't know if it was real or some trick, but I am pretty sure that bear was

chasing me."

Dozens of students reported similar experiences which sent them scattering in all directions. The minor injuries came from being trampled by others fleeing from the scene, turned ankles and other scratches and bruises from falling. Two students had worse luck, however, as they fled from the alleged spirits into oncoming traffic on Bellflower Boulevard where they were struck by cars. At press time, doctors still weren't able to supply any more information than that the students were in critical condition.

The incident raised some questions about possible hallucinogenic drug use during the ceremony, but participants and organizers flatly denied any such substances being used at the scene, which, of course, raises the question: did the students really see ghosts, or were they imagining things?

Chapter Four

After reading the article, I took a big gulp of the coffee and looked at Mack. "What do I do? What he's doing is wrong. If I go rushing in to clean up his mess, then he's going to just keep doing what he's doing."

Mack started chuckling.

"What's so funny?"

"I remember those exact words coming out of my mother's mouth when I was about six or seven years old and had hit a baseball through the living room window for the second time. I felt awful because I knew it was expensive, but I hadn't done it on purpose. I thought my mother and father would kill me, but they did worse. They didn't get angry at me, but they did make me go with them to buy the new glass and made me help fix it. I never hit another ball through that window."

"So, you're saying that Blue's sort of like a misguided kid?"

"Who said I was misguided? I just hit a ball through the window. Lots of kids do that."

"You think I should help him out?"

"That's up to you, but go talk to the boy, like you did with Carla and Michael. Two sides to every story, right?"

"I wish you had memory problems."

"Ghosts rarely have memory problems," he grinned.

"So I've noticed." I finished off my cup of coffee and started back toward the front room. I could hear Blue and Julie talking in hushed tones. Blue was all for leaving and Julie was keeping him there. She was talking me up as being the best, which felt good, and I considered holding back and not interrupting her.

"So, Blue, tell me a little more about yourself," I began, sitting down on the couch and tucking my feet up underneath me.

I saw a slight grin on Julie's face and heard her project her thought into my head. *Thank you.*

"What do you mean?" Blue asked. Telling me about himself, evidently, surprised him.

"I have to know a little bit more about a

person's background before I can really help them."

"You're going to help me?"

"I didn't say that, however, if I'm going to help you, then I'm going to need to know your background." I decided to give him a little push. "I know that your mother named you after the place you'd been conceived; the backseat of a Ford Fairlane."

If it was physically possible, I think his lower jaw would have actually hit the floor, like in the cartoons. "That was a running joke in our family when I was growing up. How did you know that?"

"I told you that I'm a real medium."

"So, why do you want to hear my story, if you can just draw it up with your gift?"

"Telling your story is good for you and I'd like to hear it from your perspective instead of mine. There's a reason you felt led to be a shaman, even if a bad one, and I want to know why."

"That's easy," he answered. "I got that from my father. He was half Chumash."

"Chumash, as in the Native American tribe indigenous to the area?"

"But your blue eyes and blonde hair?" I asked.

"Postman," he grinned. I had to admit that

the dimples in his cheeks were sort of cute.

Pauline!

"Another running joke?" I asked, ignoring Mack's objection to my earlier thought.

"Yep. We know for sure that it wasn't true."

"Of course you do, otherwise it wouldn't have been a joke."

"That's true too."

"Go ahead. I promise not to interrupt anymore." I made the motion of zipping my lips.

"I grew up listening to my father telling the stories that had been passed down through his family. I could have sat and listened to him for hours. I did, whenever he had the time to do it. He worked a lot and most of the time he wasn't home. When he was home, he was so tired that he rarely had the energy to tell stories."

I glanced at Mack. It wasn't a new story; we'd all been through it.

"I'd started visiting my grandfather a lot. He lives up near San Lucas. He took me to see the Scorpion tree in the Santa Lucia Mountains and to see the rock paintings in the Carrizo Plain. I began to feel connected to my roots in a powerful way."

Blue paused and sighed heavily before beginning again.

"I lost my father to an aggressive form of cancer in the spring of my first year at San Jose

State. The summer after he died, I spent my entire summer break in the Carrizo Plain and the Santa Lucia Mountains. I started to feel the power that came from my ancestors in those places. That was when I learned the drumming. At first, I just did it for myself, but once I realized the power that the spirits gave, I started doing it for more and more people. I quit studying at San Jose and started drumming full time. I was actually surprised by the overwhelming response. I'm not getting rich off of it, but I make a decent living."

"Do you still feel that connection with your ancestors when you drum?" I'd gotten the sense when I'd been at the detox spa that he wasn't entirely into what he was doing. I could also sense that regret in him as he sat in front of me and told his story.

"Not like I used to," he sighed. "Especially now. I don't know what's happening. I don't understand why those same spirits who had been bringing power before, now seem to be on the attack. Could it be the group drumming?"

"What do you mean?" I asked, though I had a pretty good idea.

"Most of what I had done before were, more or less, performances. I did a few small groups, but Briar Hills was the first time that I had done a drumming with a large group."

"And you didn't get a hint from that?" I asked. The Blue's Clues analogy that I'd thought of when I was at the spa returned. "Was the drumming at Cal State L.B. the same?"

"Yes," he replied. "Most of them were Native Americans, though. That's the part that really has me messed up."

"Why would the spirits attack natives?" His eyes pleaded for an answer.

I didn't have an answer. And after what had happened with Amanda after Briar Summit, I didn't want to find an answer. I didn't often run from ghosts, but I was running from these Native American Spirits. They were well beyond my understanding of things.

"I've got a simple solution for you, Blue," I began. "Stop doing the group drumming until you understand this stuff better and protect yourself from it."

"It might already be too late," he replied. "I don't think the spirits at Cal State L.B. are going back to wherever they came from."

"And you think that I'll help you send them back?" I asked. I wanted nothing to do with Blue's problem. I'd already dealt with the problem before. It wasn't pretty. I gave a very short reply before retreating for more coffee. "No."

Chapter Five

"You know," Julie's voice startled me. She'd followed me into the kitchen when I'd retreated for coffee. "I really thought that the phone call a couple of days ago was coming from the new Pauline. You know, the one who had turned over a new leaf, was ready to make a change; not the selfish one."

"The selfish one?" I turned around with my full coffee mug. I had been longing for that little bit of medicating that the shot of Captain Morgan provided. I was craving it in a big way when I realized that Julie and I were about to have it out. I didn't want to fight with her, but sometimes that's what it took to fix things. "Why is it selfish of me to say no to something that is extremely dangerous?"

"I thought your purpose was to help people; the living and the dead, is what I remember you saying," Julie replied.

She hadn't listened to the part about it being dangerous. I decided to repeat it for her. "Did you hear me say that this is extremely dangerous? I've dealt with a spirit from these people before. It was terrifying and it forced me to do something very extreme. People lost their lives at the tail end of that issue and I almost lost Mack too. So, excuse me if turning away Blue's Cl…" I stopped myself before I finished the word. It wasn't fair to be making derogatory remarks about Blue.

"You've done dangerous things before without hesitation," she responded. "Talking to those drug dealers certainly wasn't safe. Do you remember that or have you forgotten that? I think you have. I think you've forgotten that and you haven't changed. You're still selfish and self-centered. You talk about changing, you tell me that you're not going to use me anymore, but here I am asking you to help me and you're saying no. Explain that to me, Pauline."

I was aware of Mack's arrival in the kitchen. He was trying to be inconspicuous, but a ghost in the room was about the same as an elephant in the room. He was staying quiet and wasn't putting thoughts into my head either. I thought it sort of strange, but I was too focused on my conflict with Julie to worry over it.

In a way, I was proud that she was standing up for herself. She was a great deal different from the timid girl who had shown up at my door when we first met. I was, however, having some trouble with the fact that her standing up for herself was directed toward me. I didn't want to be having a confrontation with her, especially since I wanted to be restoring our friendship, but caving in and doing something that could get us all killed was a pretty significant sacrifice to make for the sake of our friendship; for any friendship.

"Julie, these native warriors are powerful. Their spirits are much more powerful than your average dead person. If you don't believe me, you can ask Mack."

I'm not in this conversation.

You are now.

"I don't want to ask Mack. I'm asking you. I don't want to put destroy our friendship completely over this, but that seems to be where this is all headed. I'm asking you for a favor. I'm asking for your help with a client. I'm asking you because you're the best at what you do. I'm asking you because you care and you'll do what needs to be done." Her plea had a sense of urgency to it that was hard to deny. "At least, those were the things that I thought I knew about you, but maybe I was wrong. I guess bringing Blue here and asking for your help was a waste of time."

A part of me wanted to just agree with her and be done with it, but doing that would be admitting the defeat of our relationship. I had to stall for time until I could come up with a better answer. I was sort of curious about how she'd come across Blue to begin with, so I started the conversation in that direction.

A diversion, Pauline? Mack's thought intruded.

Yes. Just leave me alone a minute. I'm trying to think. I was shocked that Mack, simply up and left the room. I hadn't asked him to leave. I had just asked him to stop getting into my thoughts. I really wanted him there, but I needed time to... That's when our earlier conversation hit me. *All I had to do is ask.* I'd asked and he'd responded. I guess I would have to be more precise about what I wanted.

"So, Blue is a client?" I asked. "How did you come across him?"

"He called in," Julie replied. "He was in a panic about what had happened at Cal State L.B. and he was looking for advice. When I heard what he needed, I knew it was well over my head, so I thought of you."

"Thanks for the confidence, but do you really understand what you're getting us into?"

"Up to this point, it looks like I'm not getting anyone but myself into it," Julie groused.

"Did you talk to Allison Lopez about this?"

"I didn't want to bother her. She's supposed to be on break, remember?"

I had to concede that point. I knew that Allison was on break. I'd interrupted that break a few days before. I didn't want that to have to happen again, but I was afraid of the Native American spirits; no, I was terrified. I knew what they could do. I was just about to respond when Blue showed up in the doorway of the kitchen.

"I, um, well, I heard you guys talking," he said. "I don't want to be the cause of any conflict here. It's bad for one's energy, you know?"

I felt horrible. He didn't need to be in the middle of our fight. I really hadn't wanted it to play out in front of him, but giving in to a dangerous request just to avoid being embarrassed was kind of stupid too.

"This has nothing to do with you, Blue," I said in a soft tone. "Please don't think that you're the cause of it."

"I am, partially, the cause of it," he replied and turned toward Julie. "I think it's better if we go."

I wanted to object. I started the thought in my head, but it never made it to my mouth. It didn't have much time to.

"We're going to go," Julie said in a tone that was just above a whisper.

I watched them go.

Chapter Six

The coffee in my mug was cold, coffee pot was empty, there was no Captain Morgan in my cupboard and I didn't have any cigarettes. Essentially, there was no escaping the fact that I had just let down the person who, at one time, had been my best friend. I collapsed into a chair at the kitchen table and continued a one-sided conversation with Julie in my mind, which justified my reasons for not wanting to get involved in Blue's problem over and over again.

"I don't blame you," Mack said, nearly making me wet my pants when he showed up suddenly.

"Mack!" I shouted. "You're going to make me wet myself and then you're going to drive me right back to drinking if you keep doing that."

Mack ignored the comment and continued with the thought that he had been starting before I interrupted him. "It's too dangerous. Who knows what sort of things he stirred up? In fact, one those spirits might have possessed him and is leading you into a trap."

"Did you think he was possessed by a spirit?" I asked. I hadn't sensed anything like that in Blue at any point. Why would Mack have brought that up?

"Well, because it is possible, right?" He had read my thought and answered it with a question. "We have to make sure that we have every single justification in place, just in case Julie returns to argue some more, right?"

"Are you mocking me?" I asked.

"I'm mocking the fact that you've continued arguing with here aftah she left," he answered.

"People died because of that warrior spirit," I asserted.

"That's not the way I remember things," he replied. "The warrior spirit had already been overcome before we went to that mansion in Hollywood."

"Yes, but if you'll recall, I was in a different body instead of my own and that was because of the warrior spirit."

"Do you think things would have turned out

differently if you had been in your own body? Would that have saved Amanda?"

"I don't know!" I was frustrated. I didn't want to get involved with those Native American spirits again. They were powerful and they frightened me and...

"Why don't you just admit that you are frightened of them and deal with that directly?" He broke into my thoughts with his question and nailed me down.

I hated having someone who could read my thoughts. I couldn't even get away with lying to myself. Lying to oneself was supposed to be sacred, wasn't it?

Mack started to laugh.

"Am I going to have to ask you to leave again?"

"Do you want me to leave?"

"No. I just..." I really didn't know what I intended to say. I wanted to be able to lie to myself and justify my fear with something rational and that was being taken away from me.

"Why does it have to be rationalized?"

"See, that's why I'm frustrated."

"Because I can hear your rationalizations?"

"Exactly!"

"Why does your fear have to be rational?"

"Because I don't want to tell Julie that I'm

afraid."

"Why not? I'm afraid."

"You're afraid?"

"Of course I'm afraid. I saw what you had to do the last time. I don't want to have to go through that again either, but is there only one way that this problem can be solved?"

"I don't know. Maybe it can be solved differently."

"If it could be solved differently, then shouldn't you try it?"

"But I don't know any other way."

"That's nevah stopped you before."

Mack was right. I'd solved plenty of problems for the dead and the living without knowing how I was going to do it at first. I'd been afraid plenty of times too, but I'd worked through that fear. To be fair to myself, those other fears hadn't been nearly as terrifying as my experience with the warrior spirit, but terror was little more than a deeper fear that was not yet understood. Maybe if I understood better, then I could bring that level of fear down a little bit.

"You could start by visiting the site," Mack suggested, stealing the thought that was just starting to form in my mind. "And get a feel for things before getting in too deep."

"I don't have to commit fully until I get a

better grip on things." I surprised myself that I had made the switch and had started rationalizing in the other direction.

"Besides, if you don't, then Julie might proceed and get herself in way ovah her head."

That thought had been all Mack's until he said it. The moment I heard his words, however, I snatched it up and it became my very own thought. I knew that Julie was less adequately equipped to try to help Blue than I was, but I also knew that she would go ahead and try. If she did, it would be disastrous. It might even get her killed. I didn't need that on my conscience.

"You'd better call her back," Mack advised.

I was pretty sure that his suggestion was going to be my next thought, but I'd gotten to the point where I wasn't even sure which thoughts were originally mine, which ones were Mack's and which were some sort of amalgamation of the two of us. Regardless of whose thought it was, I was already reaching for my phone, but then I hesitated.

"What do I say?"

"Why don't you just start by telling her that you thought it ovah and that you want to help?"

"And then what?"

"And then tell her the truth. Tell her you are afraid."

Being vulnerable, when Julie had looked up to me as the expert, had seemed like an injustice to her. In reality, as I considered what Mack said, it was actually more just to be honest. With that thought in my mind, I pressed the speed dial number for Julie on my cell and then felt my heart begin to race with all sorts of fears. What if she didn't answer? What if she yelled at me? What if she turned me down?

"Yeah, what's up?" Her voice broke into my thoughts as she answered the call. It was pretty obvious that she was still angry with me.

"I've been giving it some thought and I think I want to help."

"Okay, so?"

"So come on back and we'll make plans on how to proceed," I replied.

"I don't think I want to come back there right now," she answered.

I took a deep breath and tried to think of what to do next.

Just press forward. Set a time to meet her and Blue at the site. Mack's thought broke into my hesitation.

"Okay," I responded, using Mack's advice. "Why don't we just meet at Cal State L.B. tomorrow and go to the site where Blue did the drumming?"

"What time?" she asked.

"11:00 in the morning?"

There was a pause and then she came back on the line. "That works for us. See you then." Julie cut off the call.

CHANEL SMITH

Chapter Seven

To assume that Julie would be suddenly thrilled because I decided to help her would have been a little too much to expect. Even I was smart enough to figure that one out without someone whispering that thought into my ear or, in Mack's case, just inserting it there.

I would have rather not included Blue, but it was a little bit difficult to keep him from coming along; after all, it was because of his mess that the visit to Cal State, Long Beach was even necessary.

With Mack sitting in the passenger's seat, we headed out to go meet up with Julie and Blue. As we were driving down the interstate, I started to wonder if other drivers took note of the fact that I was chattering to and occasionally turning to look at an empty passenger's seat.

We could avoid that problem and talk like this, Mack suggested. "Or we can just continue. Since that tooth thingy that you stick in your ear came along, everyone appears to be chattering with no one anyway. I doubt anyone notices."

"You're probably right," I chuckled. "I've actually answered people who were talking on their 'tooth thingy' in the grocery store."

I'd done a little bit of research about what we were going to visit on the Cal State, Long Beach campus. The site, called Puvungna, was said to have been an ancient village and burial site populated by the Tongva natives. It was said to have once included a spring that had long-since dried up or seeped into a nearby creek, whose channel had been redirected to the tastes of campus maintenance department.

Attempts had been made to develop the area, but the Tongva natives that still lived in the Los Angeles area had prevented the sacred grounds from being disturbed. Though there weren't a large number of Tongva people still in the area, the National Registry of Historic Places and the courts had continued to stall any development.

"Puvungna!" Mack shouted as we pulled into the parking lot on the southwest corner of the Cal State, Long Beach campus.

"Mack!" I snapped. "Why do you insist on

startling me? Are you trying to speed up bringing me to your world by giving me a heart attack?"

"Actually, no," he laughed. "It's just a fun sounding name that seems like it ought to be shouted, like, 'Geronimo,' or whatever it was those ninja turtles used to say."

"Cowabunga," I replied.

"Yeah, that."

It was hard to disagree with him and I couldn't help smiling in spite of the "motherly" lecture I'd just delivered. We drove to a parking space, parked and got out of the car; me by opening the door and Mack by going through it. I'd taken less than three steps away from my car when Blue and Julie pulled into the parking lot and sped toward a parking space next to ours. They were in a Mitsubishi Spider convertible that was, believe it or not, blue in color. *The drumming business must be pretty lucrative.*

Mack's thoughts popped into my head. *What I wouldn't give for a chance to try that thing out.* He hovered over to give the car a good going over. It was then that I noticed the vanity tag: *DRMRBLU*.

"Hey, Miss Pauline," Blue said as he pulled himself up and over the car door without bothering to open it. "Thanks for taking this on. I sure hope we can get this problem fixed."

"I'm just taking a look around to get a feel for the place. It's not a guarantee that I can or am willing to do anything."

"I understand," he replied. "Still, it's a start, right?"

His positive attitude was catching and he was right; it was a start. I smiled and agreed with him. "It's a start."

Though Julie greeted me, I could tell that she was still nursing her grudge against me. I decided that my best approach was to remain professional.

He led us out of the parking lot and across an open area, not more than 30 or so strides, to a cluster of about a dozen trees and some brush. "Here we are. This is Puvungna."

"This is it?" I asked. There was no sign to indicate the place. I guess I'd expected to see one of those placards with the history of the place set in a slab of concrete or something, but there was nothing. More shocking was the fact that I could only feel a very small energy presence. It was hardly the ghost central that I was expecting to encounter. In fact, if I didn't know better, I'd have guessed that we'd just wandered out into an empty pasture on somebody's ranch.

"This is it," he replied. "I was expecting more the first time I saw it too."

"A sign or something, you know?" I frowned. After doing the research and learning the story behind the place and its significance to the Tongva people, I have to admit that I was pretty disappointed. Was this the best that the State of California and the National Registry of Historic Places could do?

"Probably the court battles have kept anyone from putting up any sort of a marker," Mack suggested, joining our group after satisfying his automotive curiosity.

Hearing him say that and noting that Julie turned to look in his direction as well, I realized that I probably ought to let Blue know that Mack was along with us. He couldn't see him or hear him, but it was sound, professional etiquette for me to do so. "By the way, Blue," I pointed out. "I did bring Mack, my live-in ghost, along."

"Julie said that you probably would." He didn't seem nearly as nervous as he had when he had come with Julie to my apartment. "I wouldn't mind getting a chance to see him."

"We can arrange that," Mack grinned.

I repeated what he said for Blue's benefit.

"Cool. So, how's this work? He can see and hear me, but I can't see and hear him?"

"Pretty much. I'll let you know what he says whenever he makes a comment."

"Yeah?" he laughed and winked at me. "Sort of like what a medium does?"

"Something like that," I laughed. I decided that working with Blue wasn't going to be as unpleasant as I'd first assumed. He was charming, seemed more intelligent than I noticed before and appeared to be genuinely concerned with doing whatever it took to help fix the problem he'd caused.

He's a good kid. Mack's thought came into my mind, agreeing with my own.

Chapter Eight

"So, what do you need to do?" Blue asked after several silent seconds ticked by and I started to stroll through the grove of trees.

"I'm just going to walk around and get a feel of the place. Just stay quiet and let me focus on the energy of the place. If I need information, I'll ask you questions. Try to be as honest as you possibly can and give as much detail as you can, okay?"

"Sounds simple enough."

Not a lot of energy after such a major event, I thought.

Sort of like the grounds after the midway left town, Mack responded.

"Where exactly did you hold the drumming?"

"We did it sort of like we did at Briar Summit," Blue answered. "I taught them the basics and then we wound through these trees before forming a circle around the grove."

"There were spectators?" I asked.

"Yes, quite a few, actually. I guess the novelty of it drew a lot of attention."

"Where were the spectators?"

"They were pretty much spread out from the parking lot to just a few paces away from the circle and they were spread out in a sort of half circle so that they could see."

I worked at creating a mental picture of how things were laid out. I was still only getting a very tiny energy reading from the area. I was baffled. Had the ghosts possessed the drummers or maybe the spectators? Had they gone somewhere else? Had they returned back to wherever they were called up from?

Mack's thoughts, responding to the questions in my mind were conspicuously absent.

You got any ideas here?

None different than yours, he replied.

What is the energy presence? Do you see a spirit of any kind?

Follow me, he replied.

I followed Mack, who was winding his way through the trees—something that wasn't really necessary, since he could just go through them.

I could feel the energy growing stronger, though it was still well below what I had expected.

Mack stopped suddenly, glanced in my direction and held up his hand. Then he started talking to someone who was out of my sight behind a tree. I could tell by his tone that whoever he was talking to was very young.

"Who have we here?" he asked.

"Mack is talking to someone," I announced.

"Can you see whoever it is?" Julie asked, suddenly more interested in what was taking place.

"Not yet," I replied. "Mack wants us to hang back for a second. I think it is someone who is very young."

"There's no reason to be afraid," Mack said, smiling broadly and squatting, as though he was trying to talk to someone who was very small and wanted to be on their level. "How did you get here all by yourself?"

"Mack is squatting down and talking to someone very small," Julie told Blue.

"Can you see Mack too?" Blue asked.

I wasn't sure if she could see what Mack was doing or if she was reading my thoughts as I watched him. In either case, her gift had advanced a great deal. No doubt, Allison Lopez had had a great deal to do with that. I was proud her and I smiled at her.

"Yes, they have, yes, she did, and no, I can't see Mack," she said aloud, responding to my thoughts and tossing a smirk in my direction.

You forgot the part about me being proud of you. Did you catch that one too?

Julie raised an eyebrow, but didn't respond mentally or verbally. She was blocking me from reading her thoughts; another skill she'd developed very well. It was probably a good thing she had; I might not have liked the things that she had been thinking about me.

Mack continued his conversation in a whispered tone and then looked in my direction, while nodding his head in my direction in order to encourage the person he was speaking to, to reveal their self to me.

"Go on," he said. "She's very kind, sort of like a grandmother."

Gee, thanks, Mack. Grandmother?

You're a little too old to be this one's mother, he replied.

I was about to raise another objection when I saw a tiny, little, ghost face slowly peering around the tree trunk in my direction.

"Oh, look who we have here," I said, beaming with joy. She was adorable. You'd have had to have been a complete idiot to think otherwise. She had a pair of large, startled eyes that also had a bit of sadness in them. The features of her face were very definitely those of a Native American and she had her hair cut in a pageboy. I thought of the Dora cartoon when I first saw her.

Blue's Clues and Dora? Mack asked.

Julie just looked at me like I'd gone out of my mind. Maybe I should be blocking my thoughts.

Don't you dare, both Julie and Mack responded, almost in unison. That was a freaky experience.

I inched forward, trying not to scare the little girl. When I advanced a little too far, her face disappeared behind the tree and I paused.

"It's okay, sweetie," I said. "I'm a friend."

"She's very nice," Mack encouraged.

"What's going on?" Blue asked.

"There's a little girl. She seems to be a native girl. Pauline is trying to approach her."

"There's a little girl? Why is there a little girl?" Blue asked.

"Spirits come in all ages, shapes and sizes, Blue," Julie responded.

"But if she's a spirit, then that means that she…" His face paled and he cut off the statement as he realized what the spirit of a little girl meant. "How sad."

"It is sad," Julie responded, stepping back

toward him.

Though I was focused on the place where I expected the little girl to reappear, I had caught that subtle but caring gesture out of the corner of my eye. It made me feel guilty for having missed that tenderness in Julie. I shook my head and tried to remain focused.

"What's your name, sweetheart?" I asked, hoping to draw her around the corner again.

I saw one check and one eye.

"There's that pretty girl's eye. Where's the other one?"

She smiled, popped her head out long enough for me to see both eyes and then drew back. I heard a tiny giggle from behind the tree and saw how Mack's face was lit up as he watched the two of us playing our little game. *I'll bet he was always great with kids.*

I wish I'd had more time to be a father and a grandfather, he responded to my thought. I could feel his sadness.

Evidently, the little girl felt his sadness too. She appeared from behind the trunk of the tree and gave him a big hug.

"Don't be sad," she said.

I started to tear up as I watched what was taking place in front of me. And to think that I'd almost missed this because I'd been afraid.

Chapter Nine

The little girl had stopped playing peek-a-boo with me and was looking me over, though still keeping her distance. I noted that her tiny ghost hand was in Mack's much larger one.

"Can you tell me your name, sweetheart?" Mack coaxed.

The little girl shook her head from side to side rapidly, grinning while she did it. "Guess."

"Sara, Lacey, Patty, Linda, Julie…" Mack started firing off names as fast as he could.

"No, no, no, no," the little girl giggled. "You're not even close."

"Rumpelstiltskin," I inserted.

The little girl stared at me like I was an alien.

"I thought for sure it was Rumpelstiltskin."

She shook her head and looked at me with a serious expression that was given away by the dancing light in her eyes. She was teasing me.

"I'm calling you Rumpelstiltskin anyway, since I don't know your name."

"What's going on?" Blue asked. "Who's this Rumpelstiltskin dude?"

"I'm trying to get the little girl ghost to tell me her name, Blue," I responded. "You remember the fairy tale about the girl that spun flax into gold?"

"Not in the list of stories I was told as a kid, sorry."

"How could you not...?" *Focus Pauline. Not important,* I reminded myself. I turned back toward the little girl and watched her as she watched Julie telling Blue the story about Rumpelstiltskin. How was it that a child had died and had not been taken to the light immediately?

"Who's that?" she asked, pointing toward Blue and Julie.

"That's Blue," I pointed toward Blue.

"Blue?" she giggled. "That's a funny name."

"It is funny, isn't it," I chuckled.

"Who's the lady?"

"That's Julie," I replied.

"That's a better name," she answered. She considered it for a moment with a serious expression. "I like that name better."

"My name is Pauline," I said. "Do you like that name?"

"It's better than Blue, but I like Julie better and Mack." She smiled up at Mack.

"I'll bet you have a pretty name too. Probably prettier than Rumpelstiltskin."

"Of course," she laughed. "Anything is better than Rumpless... better than the one you said."

"I agree," I wrinkled my nose. "Rumpelstiltskin isn't a very pretty name."

She kept staring at Julie. It was an intense stare, like she was studying everything about her and committing it to memory.

"You have an admirer, Julie," I said. "She's really checking you out."

"Oh, I wish I could see her. I can sort of feel her presence, but not much else."

"Trust me, she's adorable." I turned to look back at the little girl. "Aren't you, Rumpelstiltskin?"

"That's not my name!" she said with some force, even for such a tiny thing.

"I'm sorry," I answered. "What is your name?"

"I'm not telling you. I'll tell her." She pointed toward Julie.

"Okay," I said. "You tell your name to

Julie."

The little girl rushed toward Julie, who couldn't see her, but could feel her coming toward her and turned to face her.

The little girl leaned in close to her and whispered in her ear. I watched Julie's eyes narrow as she concentrated on the spirit that was all but touching her.

"Ahau?" Julie said, not certain if she'd heard correctly.

The little girl giggled and nodded her head rapidly.

"Your name is Ahau?" Julie repeated.

"Ahau," the little girl repeated. There was a tiny difference in the way she pronounced the last two letters.

Julie repeated the name more like the little girl had pronounced it. I was impressed.

"Man, I wish I could see what's going on," Blue said.

"Me too," Julie responded.

"Well, at least you can feel and hear it," he replied.

I glanced at Mack, who was sitting quietly and watching us. There was a wistful look in his eyes.

I winked at him, knowing what he was feeling.

"How did you get here, Ahau?" I asked.

"Quaoar sent me," she replied as if it was no big thing.

"Quaoar?" I asked.

"Quaoar," Ahau repeated.

"What about Quaoar?" Blue asked. His expression was grave and he was studying me intensely.

"Does that name mean something to you?"

"Of course it does," he said. "He's a deity of the Chumash, the Tongva and the other natives who lived along the Pacific Coast."

I watched Ahau, who had taken a new interest in Blue when he started talking about Quaoar.

"Keep going," I said. I wanted to see what sort of reaction Ahau was going to have toward Blue.

"Quaoar," he began, "would be similar to Jesus. In fact, when the Padres, who established the missions here, were teaching about Jesus, they related the two. Quaoar is a creator deity, who is sort of like a prophet, but is also a savior. He was the one who came along and restored order after Weywot, a tyrannical deity, had created chaos among the people and killed many of them."

Ahau's face was radiant as she listened to Blue and smiled at him.

"How'd he do?" I asked Ahau.

"I think he knows a lot about Quaoar. Maybe someday he can really, know him," she replied.

I repeated what she had said to Blue. I watched his face turn pale once more. "She really said that?"

"She really said that," I replied.

Julie confirmed with a nod of her head.

"You like him, don't you, Julie?" Ahau grinned.

I could have sworn that Julie could see Ahau. She was so tuned into the presence of the girl that she was looking right at her when she blushed, but did not reply.

Was there something brewing between Julie and Blue?

Focus, Pauline. You are not playing matchmakah.

"Ahau, why did Quaoar send you?"

"I have to find the queen who would know how to restore order," she said, almost like she was discussing going to the grocery store for a carton of milk.

"The queen?" I asked. I turned and looked at Blue.

Blue shrugged.

"Who is the queen?" I asked. "Where can we find her?"

"Quaoar said that I would meet someone

who would know where to find her. I've already met that someone."

"Who?" I asked.

"Julie," she responded.

"I don't know who the queen is," Julie responded.

"Of course you do," Ahau beamed. "Your friend will tell you."

"Oh, I wish I could see you," Julie responded. "Your presence is very sweet, but I wish I could see you."

"You can see me, silly," Ahau giggled. "But you'll want to cover your eyes a little bit, I'm pretty bright. You too, Blue."

"Cover your eyes, Blue," Julie warned.

"Huh? Okay, why?" Blue responded, covering his eyes.

Ahau started to glow until she took on the form of a brilliant, white light.

"Wow!" Julie said. "You are adorable and bright too."

"Dude!" was all Blue managed to spit out.

Ahau stayed brilliantly lit for several seconds and then returned to her spirit form.

"How did you do that?" I asked.

"Easy," Ahau replied. "I'm an angel. Bye now!"

She hugged and kissed Julie, and then disappeared.

CHANEL SMITH

Chapter Ten

"You swear that you have no idea how she did that?" I asked.

"Dahling, I'm as baffled as you are," Mack replied. "She vanished from my sight the same as yours. And, I hate to point out that you've asked me that same question more than a dozen times in the last two days."

He was right. I had been hounding him about it. It was beyond me how Ahau had vanished the way she did. Up until that point, I thought I knew pretty much everything there was to know about the paranormal world. A spirit could, given my terra firma limitation, disappear from my view, but they couldn't disappear from Mack's. The fact that Ahau had was unraveling the neat little ball of string that made up my medium understanding.

"Could it be because she is an angel?" I asked.

"Twenty-seven," Mack replied.

"Twenty-seven?" My brow was wrinkled with confusion.

"That's the twenty-seventh time you've asked me that."

"You're counting?"

"No."

"How do you know it's the twenty-seventh time?"

"An estimate."

"No exaggeration?"

Mack shrugged.

I was on my second cup of Joe for the morning and had read through the black and white funnies. I didn't really get into them that morning because my mind was otherwise detained. I was hooked on Blue's case. Besides the appearance of Ahau and the baffling enigma she'd left behind, her glowing and then vanishing act, the mystery of what became of the spirits was troubling me as well. Unlike the neat ball of string that represented my medium understanding, Blue's case was a wadded up mess.

The only question that was really answered, where Ahau was concerned, was the reason why she hadn't been taken to the light immediately, which is what always happens to children when they die. Though she'd appeared to be one, initially, she'd actually been an angel and she'd been sent to contact Julie. As a child, she was the perfect draw for Julie's attention and there had been an immediate connection between them. But Julie had no idea who the queen was or which friend would know who the queen was.

I smiled as I wondered if she had given Blue as hard of a time in trying to figure out the riddle as I had given Mack.

"I hardly think so," he said, answering my thought with a stern expression on his face. "No doubt, Julie is not as abusive to him as you are to me."

"I cannot believe you just said that. Especially after all I've done for you."

A smile broke over his face and it became obvious that he was having fun with me. Somehow I'd missed the twinkle that was usually in his eyes when he pulled a fast one on me. Either I was losing my touch or he had found some new way of hiding that twinkle so that he didn't give his jokes away.

"I'll nevah tell," he laughed.

"Would you stop answering my thoughts?"

"Do you want me to leave?"

"No. I want you to help me recap and go through this again."

Mack sighed, looked skyward and muttered, "When will the light come again?"

"Tough luck, pal," I responded. "You promised to wait until we could go to the light together. I'm afraid you're stuck with me until I keel over."

Mack started singing what sounded like a hymn. "Showers of blessing, showers of blessing we need: mercy-drops round us are falling, but for the showers we plead."

Though I waited, enjoying his rich, baritone voice as he sang, I couldn't help my response. "Smart ass."

He giggled a little bit and then turned serious. "We've been over this several times, but there is really only one paht that concerns us and one paht that concerns Julie. For our paht, we have to ask what became of the spirits. But Julie has to come up with the identity of the queen."

"That's a little oversimplified, but okay, sure. Of course, you didn't add that before Julie can come up with the identity of the queen, she has to identify the friend who knows about the queen."

"I didn't think that I needed to state the obvious," he replied.

"Okay, so where did those spirits go?" I posed.

"They were probably afraid that you'd hound them with questions and you scared them off."

"Be serious!"

"I am being…" He stopped himself and started chuckling softly.

"What?"

"Listen to us."

"Listen to what?"

We sound just like an old married couple.

In spite of myself, I had to laugh. He was absolutely right. I suppose we'd interacted that way all along, but a lot of the banter that took place before was somehow connected to me being a "bazo" as he used to call me. Since then, the banter had changed. It wasn't bad, but we did need to tone it down a little bit or one of us would get pissed off.

"Message received," he responded.

"Let's take a break from this discussion for a few minutes, okay?"

"Sure," Mack shrugged.

I turned to the obits, taking a long draught from my tepid coffee but to add a dab of coffee to warm what was in my mug before I started reading. I glanced at Mack, who was pouring over the sports pages, and smiled before sitting down again.

"Well, now," I chuckled. "We might have just caught a break in our case."

"Who died?"

"Joseph David Timmons," I replied.

"And he is?"

"One of the students who was hit by a car while feeling from the drumming at Cal State, Long Beach," I replied, and then started a question. "You don't suppose…"

"I'm already on it, my love," he said. "Wanna see my vanishing act?"

"Impress me."

It wasn't bad; actually, he did it pretty quickly. Of course, it helped that he was sitting/hovering over a chair that was against the wall and all he really had to do was propel himself backward. A second later, he peered around the corner of the window.

"Bravo!" I called out, applauding. "Bravo!"

Chapter Eleven

"May I present Joe Timmons," Mack announced formally.

"What the hell, dude?" Mack's somewhat unwilling guest objected when he was pushed through the door and into my front room.

"Hey Joe," I smiled. I'd been considering the joke for a while. I finally used it. "Welcome to Ghost Central."

"Ghost what?" he asked.

"Never mind," I said, realizing that Joe was too much of a novice as a ghost to deal with my dry sense of humor. "How are you doing?"

"To be honest," he began, "I think I'm dead and I'm still trying to figure a lot of things out."

"It can be like that for a day or two, but with any luck, you'll be able to go to the light and won't have to deal with it for very long. It's sort of confusing until you get the hang of it. Just ask Mack."

Joe turned and looked over his shoulder at Mack, who was hovering just behind him and a little bit above him. "So, this guy is like a ghost goon?"

"Something like that," I replied.

A ghost goon? Mack responded in my head.

"And you are?"

"I'm Pauline," I answered. "I'm a medium."

"Mediums are like people that do séances, talk to the dead and stuff like that, right, dude?"

"Stuff like that," I replied.

"Cool."

I was forming my first question when Joe interrupted me.

"So, like some person that isn't dead wants to talk to me then, like my mom or my sister or something?"

"No, actually, just me," I replied.

"Why do you want to talk to me? I don't even know you, dude."

Being called dude was a little bit unsettling for me. All of my life, I'd grown with dude only being used to refer to the male of the species. I considered correcting him, but there wasn't much point. I considered that old adage about old dogs and new tricks. When applied to someone who was dead…

Focus, Pauline, Mack's voice said inside my head.

"Can I ask you some questions about how you died?" I asked.

"Not much to it, really. I got hit by a car."

"Before that?"

"I was running and ran into the street."

"Why were you running?"

"There was a bear chasing me, dude." His eyes got even bigger when he said that.

"Did the bear catch you?"

"I don't think so, dude. I was hauling some ass."

I wanted to laugh, but a voice inside my head—either mine, Mack's or a combination of the two—told me to stay in control.

"You're pretty sure he didn't catch up to you, maybe crawled inside your body and made you run out into traffic?" I was too late in realizing that, by the way I worded the question, I was putting a suggestion in his head. I was about to chastise myself for leading the witness when he responded.

"No, definitely not, dude, he didn't catch up with me. Running out into traffic was all me. I was scared. I was just trying to get away and I had no idea where I was going. I didn't care."

I could tell he wanted to talk about what had

happened, so I decided to let him. Maybe I'd glean some additional information out of him. "Why don't you start from the beginning?"

"Okay, well, I was born in Glendale..." he started.

"Not that beginning," I interrupted. "Just give me what happened at Cal State the day they had the drumming."

"Oh, okay," he laughed. "I thought you meant the beginning, beginning, like my beginning, dude."

"It's Pauline." The dude had gotten to me enough to make me actually correct him.

"What, dude?"

"Never mind. Just tell me about the drumming."

"It was actually pretty cool at first. That rhythm was sort of like a drug, you know, dude? He showed us how to do it and then we followed along behind him in a line and we walked around in the trees of that old burial site or whatever it was..."

"Wait a second," I interrupted, and then looked up at Mack. "I thought Blue told us that only the Native American students were drumming."

"I am a Native American student," Joe replied. "I'm one-quarter Cherokee. I got a scholarship because of it."

"But you said you were born in Glendale."

"I was."

"Cherokees come from Oklahoma," I pointed out.

"Dude, that's where my mom was from! Small world, huh? Are you from Oklahoma?"

"No." I was regretting having interrupted him.

"That's good, because Oklahoma sucks," he laughed. "My dad always said that. He was from Texas. He had this joke about why Texas doesn't fall off into the Gulf of Mexico."

"That's okay. I don't need to hear it."

"Because Oklahoma sucks," he laughed. "Get it."

"I get it."

"Oklahoma's sucking keeps Texas from falling off into the Gulf of Mexico."

"Tell me about the drumming." It came out with a little more force behind it than I intended it to. I tried to sweeten it with the magic word. "Please?"

"Yeah, sure, dude, but you're the one who asked about Oklahoma, don't get your panties in a wad."

Can ghosts be stoned? I asked Mack.

I think this one had fried his brains long ago.

"Where was I?"

"You were following along in a line and drumming…" I prompted.

"Yeah, and then we made a circle. It was a pretty good circle; we were all the way around that bunch of trees. There were an ass load of people watching us too. Dude, I never felt so powerful in my life. That's what the drummer dude said would happen and it did. I felt like I could pull a tree up by its roots and stuff. I was like, 'A*aaaagggghhhh*, I'm powerful, dude.'"

I'd felt that same power at Briar Summit right before everything went horribly wrong.

"I started seeing faces of these Indian dudes, right? Not the ones with the dot on their heads and wrap a towel around their heads, but the ones that wear feathers in the hair, you know, dude?"

"Yes, I know. What happened next?" I was ready to get the interview over with before I lost my mind.

"I got really scared, because those dudes turned into animals and that's when the bear started chasing me. I threw that little drum and started hauling ass."

"You didn't notice what happened to any of the other animals or any other of the Indian dudes?" I couldn't believe that I had actually used his own words. I caught a wink from Mack. He hadn't missed it.

"I was running for my life, dude. I didn't see anything but the bear that was chasing me."

"Okay. Thanks," I said. "Mack can take you back to where he found you so you can wait for the light to come."

"Sure, dude, no prob. Did I help you?"

"Yeah, sure, you helped, thanks," I replied.

"Let's go, dude," Mack grinned, pushed Joe through the door and then looked back at me. "I'll be back soon so we can go track down those Indian dudes."

I was wishing that I still smoked so that I could throw an ashtray at him.

CHANEL SMITH

Chapter Twelve

Mack and I had arrived at the same conclusion by the time that he'd returned from taking Joe back to where he'd found him. The spirits hadn't possessed any of the students participating or observing the drumming. If they had been possessed, then there certainly would have been some reports of other strange things taking place on the Cal State, Long Beach campus. There had been no other news, though Joe's death made the paper along with a report that the other critical student was on his way to a slow recovery.

What we still hadn't figured out was where those spirits went. The fact that there were no energy footprints when we'd visited before was a little bit odd, especially after a paranormal event on the scale that had been described by Joe, by Blue and by the witness accounts that were reported in the paper. If they hadn't possessed anyone and weren't present at Puvungna, then where were they? Was it all over? Was there nothing more for us to do?

Mack and I were in the process of trying to answer those questions when my phone rang. I looked at the caller ID, noted that Allison Lopez popped up on the screen and looked at Mack, who had already read the question in my mind. *Allison Lopez is calling?*

"Hi Allison," I said after pressing the button to connect the call. "What's up?

Dude, Mack added into my mind.

I glared at him and he laughed.

"Pauline," she said. "How are things in sunny Southern California?"

"Sunny and warm, just like always."

"I've got something urgent I need to discuss with you."

"Sure." Going straight to the point was a little bit odd, even for Allison. I wrinkled my brow as I tried to anticipate what she was about to discuss with me.

"We have been overloaded with strange phenomenon taking place all over L.A. and the metro area. Was there some sort of major event there? Our phones are ringing off the hook and we're barely able to keep up with it."

"What sort of phenomenon are we talking?" I already had a gut feeling of what she was about to tell me.

"Spirits, Native American spirits, the spirits of wild animals, that sort of thing."

"Like, bears, wolves, cougars, rattlesnakes and ravens?" I asked.

She didn't respond for a few minutes and then said. "Those are what are being reported. Do you know something?"

"I do," I answered. "About all I can tell you is that we're working on it."

"Can you give me some background? Maybe I can help."

I filled her in on everything that we knew. When I had finished, I wondered for a moment if she had hung up.

"Are you still there?"

"I'm still here. I wish I had some sort of answer for you. I'll talk to Julie about the queen, but no one is ringing a bell with me at the moment. I can't think of who her friend might be, but that whole thing is pretty enigmatic as it is. I think I'd go back to the site and see if you could get a different reading or talk to Ahau again. Maybe you can pick up some more clues?"

"I think that was the conclusion that Mack

and I were just about to come to."

"Do you need my help?"

"Let us see what we can come up with. I hate to disturb your break."

"What break?" she laughed.

I really didn't want to disturb Allison's time off. Besides, I suddenly had a premonition that told me that Blue's case wasn't just about solving the issue of spirits on the loose. There was a greater purpose; something that was necessary for Julie and me to do together. I told Allison as much.

"In that case," she replied, "you two tend to business, but keep me in mind if you get in over your heads and need a hand."

"We will," I responded.

I disconnected the call and turned toward Mack.

"A greater purpose?" he grinned.

"Did you put that thought into my head?"

"Wasn't me," he replied. "But I agree."

"She hasn't been altogether thrilled with being around me the last couple of times."

"Is that why you've backed off on bothering her about the queen and focused on driving me out of my mind?"

"Could be," I said, pressing the speed dial button for Julie on my cell phone. "Besides, I have to harass someone and you can take it."

"What's up?" Julie asked as she answered the phone.

"I talked to Allison and she suggested that we go back to the site and see if we can't get some more clues." By inserting Allison, it didn't seem like I was being too much in charge. "When can you and Blue meet us there?"

There was a pause. I could hear a conversation taking place. Was she asking him directly? Was he there? Were they...?

"We can meet you there at 11:00. Does that work?"

I looked at the clock. It was almost 9:00. I'd have to hurry a little to get ready, but it was doable. "How about 11:30?"

"That'll work. See ya, then."

The call disconnected. Things hadn't improved a great deal between the two of us. We were civil, but there wasn't a lot of warmth.

Give it some time, Pauline. Rome wasn't built in a day.

Again, I wasn't sure whose thought it had been, my own or Mack's. But I tucked it away and headed toward the bathroom to start getting ready.

Mack and I arrived a little bit before 11:30, but had barely gotten out of the car when Blue's blue Spider pulled into the parking lot and roared to a stop beside my car. I watched the two of them carefully. Had they become a couple?

What if they have? Mack's question interrupted my thoughts.

Nothing, I'm just wondering.

I'm wondering if I can take that car for a spin.

You can't drive! You're a ghost for God's sake!

I still want to sit behind the wheel. Mack waited for Blue to get out of the driver's seat and then hovered down into the driver's seat.

"You don't mind if Mack checks out your car do you?" I asked Blue.

"He wants to check out my car?"

"He's sitting behind the wheel right now. Well, not really sitting."

Blue looked toward the driver's side of his car, trying to decide how he felt about a ghost sitting there. "Cool," he said, grinning and nodding his head.

In that very moment, Mack used latent power from something in the car and revealed himself.

"Jesus!" he exclaimed, jumping back a little at the sight of Mack. "He really is there."

Mack waved at him and then disappeared.

Chapter Thirteen

The energy of Puvungna was much different than it had been a few days before. Where there had only been the very small force of energy from Ahau the first time, there was an overpowering and sinister energy as we approached the grove. I looked toward Julie, whose expression had turned from quiet contentment —probably had something to do with whatever was going on with her and Blue—to one of gravity and a little bit of fear. I noticed that she reached out for Blue's hand.

"I'm not liking this very much," Mack commented.

I wasn't liking it much either. In fact, I was starting to relive the terror that I'd had when facing the warrior that had possessed Amanda.

"Maybe this was a bad idea."

"What?" Blue asked. "What's going on? What are you feeling?"

I started to answer, but Julie cut in.

"There's a very powerful and very sinister presence here," she responded in a low tone. With a slight tremor in her voice, she asked me a question. "Do you see anything, Pauline?"

"Not yet. Mack?"

"There's someone behind the trunk of that big tree to the left," he replied. "I can't see him, but I can feel him. He's very powerful."

"The big tree to the left," I said aloud so that Julie and Blue would be kept in the loop.

As I turned in that direction, I began to get a stronger sense of the spirit's presence as well.

"What do you want?" he snapped, before stepping out from behind the tree.

He was much like the warrior that I'd battled before, but seemed to be even more powerful. He glanced toward Mack, smirked a little, examined both Julie and myself from head to toe with slow precision and then his eyes focused on Blue. "Why did you bring him here?"

"We brought him because he feels responsible for what happened and wants to set things right." I attempted to speak with more confidence than I really felt. There wasn't really any point in it, because the spirit would be able to tell that I was afraid of him anyway.

"He is a heretic of his people!" the spirit bellowed and then hissed through clenched teeth. "He must be put to death."

Although I knew that Julie could not see or hear the spirit, I noticed that she moved over in front of Blue. She had powerful senses, which she had been developing a great deal.

"What has he done?" I asked, trying to draw his attention back to me. I wasn't comfortable with the way that the spirit was looking at Julie as though she had just issued him a challenge.

"Who is he?" Blue asked, only hearing my side of the conversation. "Me? Is he talking about me?"

"He is," I said quietly.

Blue shouldered his way past Julie and stepped forward. "I didn't mean it, really, I didn't. I didn't know what I was doing. I was just doing what I learned from my grandfather's people. I didn't mean to upset anyone or anything."

"Silence him!"

"That's probably enough, Blue," I said. "I think you're just making him angrier."

"Tell me what's going on," he said.

"Well, he is calling you a heretic of your people and calling for you to be put to death."

I'd learned as a medium that failing to tell the entire truth, however uncomfortable it might be, was never a good idea.

"Whew," Blue said, feeling the weight of the accusation upon his shoulders. He whispered his apology again. "I'm sorry."

"If it makes any difference," I said, stepping forward with a confidence that I still didn't have. "He's agreed to stop doing the drummings."

Easy, Pauline, Mack warned.

"Pauline," the spirit grinned and then hissed through his clenched teeth once more. "You have no idea what sort of power you're dealing with here."

The statement was mostly made in order to let me know that he had picked up on the mental conversation between Mack and me. We could usually block those conversations and keep them between ourselves.

"Are you responsible for the spirits that are causing chaos throughout the city?" I asked.

"I am their ruler, yes, but Blue, there—" he jerked his head toward Blue "—is the one responsible for setting them loose. It was his heresy that awakened them. I can't say that I'm disappointed. I've waited for such an opportunity for a very long time."

In spite of my fear, I tried to focus on the

content of what he was saying. I focused on one question. My job as a medium typically involved resolving a conflict between the living and the dead. Understanding the conflict was the first step. "How has he committed a heresy?"

"I know what you're doing, Pauline," he laughed. "It won't work. There can be no restoration until enough blood has been shed and it will only end with the shedding of his blood."

"I want to know about the heresy." I wasn't sure if it was a good idea to press the issue, but I wasn't letting it go.

"You're playing a dangerous game, Pauline, but I'll answer your questions, because I'm amused by them. First, Blue is not pure in his own people. He is neither Chumash nor English. He is a lie of two peoples. He ought not to be sharing the power of one with the other. Second, he brought together more liars from numerous peoples; liars just like himself. He led them in a sacred ceremony, not once, but twice. Third, this last time that he committed this heresy, he did it at a sacred site, even after he had been warned."

I started to form my next question.

"Aren't you going to pass along my words to him? He fashions himself as a seer and a shaman and yet, he cannot see the spirits he calls nor hear their voices when they speak."

I related the spirit's words aloud so that Blue could hear them, believing that to not do so would anger the spirit further. When I had finished, I asked my next question without waiting. I was afraid to stop, because I was afraid I wouldn't have the nerve to continue if I didn't.

"How much bloodshed will be enough?" I asked, not really wanting to know, but knowing that I needed to have some idea of what we were up against. I was trembling.

"There will be enough when I say there is enough," he snapped. "Did you come here to stop me?"

I could see his anger beginning to boil and I thought it best to divert the challenge until we could come up with a better understanding of what we were dealing with.

"No, we came here to talk to Ahau and find out more about the queen," I responded.

"The queen!" he bellowed. A powerful glow came up in his eyes.

I braced myself, extending my hands to ward off the blow that I knew was coming and screamed to the others. "Run! Now!"

Chapter Fourteen

I awakened with a start. My spirit, my mind, and my body were still in battle mode, though everything had suddenly gone black for a time before light appeared again and I was staring up at the ceiling above my very own bed. I'm not sure how I got back to my apartment or who put me on my bed.

You're okay, dahling. I heard Mack's reassuring voice in my head.

What happened?

He hit you pretty hard.

The Indian spirit?

Yes.

"Julie and Blue?" I sat up, suddenly.

"We're okay," Julie responded from the chair beside my bed.

When I turned my head and focused my eyes on her, she responded to the next question in my head. "Blue's out in the front room, pacing."

"So, everybody is okay, then," I sighed.

"Yes," Mack and Julie both answered at the same time.

"Blue?" Julie called out over her shoulder and then turned back to me. "He's been pretty worried about you. He blames himself and he's pretty upset."

I tried not to let the thought that popped into my mind happen, especially since Julie had started becoming so adept at reading my thoughts, but it came in anyway. *He ought to blame himself; he caused all of this.*

There is no sense going there, Pauline.

From Julie's reaction, or lack thereof, I realized that she hadn't caught my thought. She turned and smiled up at Blue as he came into the room.

"Pauline," he gasped. "I'm so glad you're okay. I'm so sorry. This is all my fault. I've really messed things up…"

"What happened?" He might have continued falling all over himself if I hadn't interrupted him. Mack was right, there was no sense rehashing how we'd gotten into the situation. We were in it and we needed to find our way out of it. I pulled myself up to a sitting position, noting that Julie had scrambled to move pillows behind me.

I looked toward Mack, who was about to start speaking before I stopped him. "I think Blue should hear this too."

Julie, knowing the process, drew the curtains closed, grabbed the remote from the nightstand, turned on the TV, muted it and then handed the remote to me. I extended it toward Mack.

"Mack's going to reveal," Julie said to Blue.

"He's going to what?"

"You're going to be able to see him in a moment," I smiled. "Do you need to sit down?"

"No, I'm go…" He started to respond, until he saw the remote moving on its own and Mack's ghostly form begin to take shape. "Maybe I better sit down."

"I'm really not that scary," Mack said with a chuckle and then added, "unless I want to be."

Blue just stared at him with wide eyes and swallowed the lump in his throat.

"He'll be alright in a minute," I grinned. "Go ahead and start telling me what happened."

"Well, when you told him that you were looking for Ahau and the queen," Mack began, "he went berserk."

"I remember bracing myself and telling everyone to run," I replied.

"Yeah, that was just before he hit you with a pretty good jolt of energy," Mack continued. "Julie and Blue had started running like you said. The spirit started aftah them, but he came up short, just as they got beyond the edge of the grove of trees. It seems that this spirit was unable to cross an invisible line."

We'd had a discussion about why some ghosts were limited to certain places and others like Mack were not, but we'd never arrived at a solution. "So, he's one who is limited," I muttered.

"It appeared so," Mack replied. "Since he couldn't cross ovah, he turned and started aftah me. Dahling, I tried to stay with you, but I ran like a frightened little girl."

"That turned out to be a good thing," Julie broke in. "Because Blue rushed back to you, picked you up and carried you out of the grove."

"Did you do that for me, Blue?" I asked.

"Um, yeah. Yeah, I did," Blue replied, trying to find his voice in spite of the fact that he was still pretty shaken by Mack's presence.

"He wasn't very happy that we slipped away from him," Mack smiled. "He roared and carried on the entire time. Anyway, Blue put you in the back of the convertible and Julie got in your car and drove it home."

I could tell by the look on his face that he'd ridden back with me and that he'd enjoyed his ride in the Spider. "You're just like a kid," I laughed.

"He was going to take you to the hospital," Julie jumped in. "But I talked him out of it."

"You were out of it the whole way back," Blue said. "I was scared pretty bad. Are you okay? I mean, really okay... or do we need to get you to the hospital?"

"I'm really okay," I replied. I was still a little bit woozy, but besides being completely drained of all energy, I didn't have any other complaints except one. "I am a little bit hungry, though."

Blue seemed to have gotten more comfortable with Mack's presence, at least, as long as he was focused on me. When he looked back up and saw Mack, sitting/hovering above the bed, he clammed up and sat back in the chair.

"Really, Blue," I laughed. "He's not going to hurt you."

"What do you want for lunch?" Julie asked. "I could send Blue out for something."

"No, need," I replied. "I whipped up some chicken salad last night in anticipation of lunch today. There's some bread and probably some chips somewhere. I don't know, just go digging around."

Julie took off, dragging Blue—who was only too eager to get away from Mack—along with her.

Mack put down the remote and stretched out beside me with his head resting on his hand as he looked into my eyes. "Are you really okay?"

"If I wasn't, then you'd already know it. It's a little hard for me to keep my own thoughts private with you around."

"That's true."

"We're still no closer, Mack," I pointed out.

"You're already worrying about this again?"

"Los Angeles and the metro area have a serious problem right now. We have to come up with a solution."

"You're a little low on energy right now," Mack pointed out.

"Okay," I grinned. "So, we'll wait until after lunch."

Chapter Fifteen

Lunch made me feel better, but I'd insisted on going into the kitchen to eat it instead of having it served to me in bed. I probably shouldn't have been embarrassed to have everyone congregated in my room after what I'd just been through, but I was. Besides, I needed to push myself forward if we were going to figure out how to fix L.A.'s enormous paranormal problem before the "bloodshed," which the spirit threatened, got out of hand.

As we enjoyed my killer chicken salad, I brought up the fact that we still had an enormous problem to solve and we weren't much closer.

"All we really know is that the spirits who are running loose in L.A. are out for blood.

Evidently, they are ruled by whoever this spirit is and he's pretty keen on getting his hands on Blue for his final sacrifice." I looked at Blue, who had been eating eagerly up until that moment. Maybe I shouldn't have mentioned that last part until he'd finished his lunch.

"So, is this the chaos that the queen is supposed to put to an end?" Julie asked.

"The queen is supposed to know how to restore order," I replied.

"Ahau said that she was supposed to find the queen who would restore order. Either I or my friend is supposed to know who this queen is. Guys, I have no idea who she's talking about. I wondered if it was Blue and I thought it might be Allison. I've gone through all of my friends and…" Julie froze suddenly. I'd say, as if she'd seen a ghost, but seeing ghosts didn't have the same effect on her as it used to have. She turned pale and then looked at me like she was pleading for forgiveness for some great sin. "Carla. I can't believe I didn't think of her first."

"Carla would know?" Mack asked, taking the words right out of my mouth; my brain, actually.

"Why would Carla know?" I asked.

"How should I know?" Julie responded.

"Who is Carla?" Blue asked.

"Carla is my soul mate," Julie responded.

She looked at me with the look someone gives when they're not sure how much more information they need to be giving away.

I just smiled.

"Cool," Blue said, standing up and reaching into his pocket for his keys. "Let's go talk to her."

I held back a laugh as I watched Julie's face sink. She wasn't going to get to avoid explaining who Carla was and I was going to get to watch her do it.

"Finish your lunch, Blue," I chuckled. "You're not going anywhere."

Julie rewarded me with a face that said, "thank you" and "you suck" at the same time.

"Sure," Blue said, sitting back down. "We can go after we eat lunch."

I was pretty sure that Mack was going to bust a gut from laughing. It wasn't helping my efforts at keeping a straight face.

"Okay," Blue said, noticing my struggle. "What am I missing?"

"For some reason, Pauline thinks it's funny that my soul mate is a spirit who has moved on beyond the light."

I have to credit Blue. He took it better than I thought he would. In fact, he took it so well that I was disappointed.

Julie smirked at me when she saw that

Blue's reaction wasn't anything like what I had geared myself up for, and then filled Blue in on Carla's story and how they had connected and become soul mates.

As Julie told the story, I relived those days when Julie and I had first met. In truth, I was starting to get choked up before she was finished. The friendship that we'd had when we'd first started and right afterward had been a very sweet and meaningful time in my life all the way up until I'd blown it. I so regretted having blown it. I'd blamed Captain Morgan, but in reality, it had been all me.

"So, she went on to the light?" he asked. "How do you talk to her?"

"Really, I just feel her presence and we share certain energies," Julie replied.

"We're going to have to call her up," I inserted. "Ask her if she knows who this queen that Ahau was talking about is?"

"I didn't know that we could call her back once she crossed over," Julie said.

"Well, it's not like I can send Mack out to fetch her, but it can be done."

"Are you sure you have the energy for that, dahling?" Mack asked.

"At this very moment? No, but if I take a nap after I finish lunch, I might," I replied. "Séances work best as close to midnight as possible anyway."

"A séance?" Blue asked. He knew what one was and his eyes widened.

"You going to be able to handle that, b... Blue?" Julie asked.

I was pretty sure by the way she reached over and touched his hand and by the way that she looked at him that she had been about to say, "babe." I smiled, knowing that Julie and Blue had something going on between them and that, for some reason, they were trying to keep it a secret. I started to tell them that I'd already figured it out, but Mack stopped me.

Pauline, mind your own business. She'll tell you when she's ready.

He was right and Julie was already changing the subject anyway. "So, Blue and I can get things set up for tonight while you rest, Pauline. Tell me where everything is so we don't have to bother you."

"I can help," Mack suggested.

"Mack said that he would help," I said. "He knows where everything is. I think he snoops around when I'm not watching him."

"How is Mack going to help if we can't see him, hear him and talk to him?" Blue asked.

Julie started giggling. "The TV and the remote? He just has to draw energy and he can reveal himself."

"He can also draw enough energy to move things," I added.

"Like turn over chairs," Julie laughed. "He used to do that all the time to get Pauline's attention before."

"Sort of like this," Mack said, giving one of my kitchen chairs a shove.

Blue jumped so high when the chair turned over that I was afraid we'd have to pry his fingernails out of the ceiling to bring him back down.

Julie, Mack and I laughed until tears were in our eyes. Blue finally joined in, realizing that he was sort of being broken into an elite fraternity.

"You better break him in right if he's going to be hanging around with us, Jules."

That was when Julie realized that I was on to them. She threw a shocked look in my direction and I winked at her as I pushed back my chair and stood.

"I'm going to go take my nap," I announced and then turned toward Mack. "Please be nice to Blue."

"Moi?"

"Vous."

Chapter Sixteen

It was dark when I awakened from my nap. The house was silent and I strained my ears to try to pick up even the slightest sound. Mack wasn't even there to greet me. The silence was a little unsettling. *I wonder where everyone went.* I kicked the blanket aside and turned to put my feet on the floor.

I did a quick search through the house, did a once over of the séance setup, being very impressed with how well they'd done, and then felt my bladder inform me that I had to take care of some other, urgent business. I was tending to that business when I heard Mack's voice on the other side of the door.

"We're back, dahling."

"I'll be right out," I replied. It was one of the

few times that it didn't bother me to have him calling to me through the door.

A few seconds after Mack's announcement, I heard Julie and Blue coming through the front door and Julie calling out to me. "I'm coming," I replied, having finished my business and reaching for the doorknob. Before I opened the door, I turned back toward the mirror and smiled at myself. "Energy, Pauline."

Julie and Blue were busy extracting the contents of several bags, placing the easily-recognizable, Chinese takeout cartons on the table.

"My God! How much food did you get?" I gasped.

"We got a little bit of everything," Julie said. "Blue knows this great Chinese place in Beverly Hills."

"Beverly Hills?" I asked. "It looks to me like you brought food from every province in China."

"Pauline, if you like Chinese," Blue beamed, "you're going to love this."

"Then I'm going to love this," I laughed. "You guys didn't really have to do this. It must have cost a fortune. What's the damage? I at least want to pay for my part."

Julie and Blue froze and looked at each other and then back at me.

"What's wrong?" I asked.

"You sort of already paid for all of it," Julie responded in a quiet voice. "Mack said…"

"Mack!" I called out. Mack was nowhere to be found. I was pretty sure that he'd gotten his misty mitts on my credit card again too. He'd already done some online shopping a couple of times.

"OMG, Pauline, I'm sorry," Julie said. "I've been thinking of you two as a couple. Blue and I were planning on paying for our part anyway."

"That's not really the point, Julie," I snapped. It wasn't directed at her, but it might have seemed like it was. "That wasn't meant for you, Jules. He seems to think that he can use my credit card whenever he wants. Mack!"

"Yes, dahling?" he replied, coming through the outside wall and into the kitchen.

"My credit card?"

"I didn't think you'd mind."

"I would have liked to have been…" I started in on giving him the what for and then stopped. Realizing that a one-sided argument between me and a ghost that the other two persons in the room couldn't see was going to be pretty strange, I cut the conversation off and then let him quite clearly read the thought in my mind. *We'll talk about this later!*

Blue was right about the Chinese food. I

loved it and I was stuffed by the time we started clearing the table and putting the leftovers in the fridge. We chatted and laughed, getting to know Blue better. Julie and I took turns telling stories about each other and all of the memories we'd made came rushing back. It was good to be laughing along with Julie again. We paused a moment and I looked across at Julie.

I've missed this.
Me too.

I looked up at the kitchen clock. "Wow! It's a quarter 'til midnight. We better go get settled in."

Blue's face paled as he pushed back his chair and started to follow us into the front room.

"It's okay," Julie said in a low tone. "You're going to love Carla."

Who couldn't love Carla?
I know, right?

We took our seats around the table. I'd set up the TV and remote so that Mack would be visible to all present and I gave a few instructions for Blue's benefit. He nodded his understanding and swallowed the lump in his throat. The first time was always a little unsettling; mostly because of there was a fear of the unknown. Of course, adding to the effects of Blue's first time experience was the presence of

Mack at the table across from him.

I started in with my summons to Carla. I felt a little bit weak, initially, but Mack's hand hovering over mine was providing some extra strength as we began to draw her spirit from beyond the veil and into our physical world. I could feel Carla's spirit, but it was the squeal of delight that she let out as she rushed to wrap her arms around Julie that told me that we'd summoned her successfully.

"Jules!"

The high-pitched screech from Carla nearly sent Blue scrambling from the room, but the combination of my hand and Julie's hand gripping him tightly, as well as his being paralyzed with fear, held him in his seat.

"Carla," Julie replied.

"I've missed you so much, Jules."

"I've missed you too."

"Hey, Pauline." She waved. "Hey, Mack."

We each responded.

"Is this him, Jules?" Carla asked.

"How did you know?"

Carla just rolled her eyes.

"Blue, I'm Carla," she said, extending a formal, ghostly hand toward him.

Blue reached out toward it. His eyes were still wide and his brow was wrinkled with confusion about shaking hands with a ghost. In a tone, which was just above a whisper, he responded. "I'm Blue."

"He's cute, Jules. No wonder you chatter endlessly about him."

"Carlaaaa," Jules said in a low tone.

"Oops. Did I let a cat out of a bag?" She giggled with delight and then moved over to hover right beside Blue. "So, Blue, tell me about yourself."

Blue had trouble finding his tongue. "Well, I…"

I decided to go to Blue's rescue, especially since we needed to get information out of Carla while the energy was strong enough. "Carla, we need your help with a problem."

"You need my help, Pauline? Do we need to rough up some drug dealers?" she giggled as she attempted a stern expression.

"Actually, we need to find out if you know the queen."

"The queen?" Carla asked. "Why would I know the queen?"

"This Native American, which we think was an angel, said that you might know who she was," Julie broke in.

"I just love angels," she said. "They're all over the place on the other side and they're so sweet."

I was afraid that we'd struck a dead end with

Carla and I was beginning to feel a little bit hopeless when she suddenly stopped chattering.

"Wait!"

"What?" Julie asked, broadening a smile that had already been impossibly broad.

"You said Native American?" Carla asked.

"Yes."

"There was this old woman who used to hang out in the corner. She always hid behind that juniper tree whenever we were walking up and down the steps. You remember seeing her, Mack, don't you?"

"I do remember her," he said, lighting up instantly.

"She introduced herself to me as Queenie."

"She did?" Mack asked. "I never saw her talking to anybody."

"She was pretty grumpy and didn't want to talk to me, but I made her do it anyway."

Carla was beginning to fade as the energy level started to go down. I knew that she would disappear soon. "Thank you, Carla."

"Don't mention it, Pauline."

"Bye, Mack. Bye, Blue. I love you, Jules."

CHANEL SMITH

Chapter Seventeen

"That was freakin' awesome!" Blue said after Carla was gone.

Julie and I grinned as we looked at each other and then back at Blue.

"I bettah go find Queenie," Mack announced, dismissing himself, and then quickly disappearing through the front door.

"What did you think of Carla, Blue?" Julie asked.

"She was freakin' awesome!"

"You should have seen your face when she squealed," Julie laughed. "If I hadn't held onto your hand so tight, I think you'd be halfway to Sacramento by now; running."

"Yeah. Pauline has a hell of a grip too," he laughed. "I couldn't have run anywhere. I was freakin' paralyzed."

"You looked pretty freakin' freaked out to me," Julie mocked.

"I was, but she was so adorable. I didn't know that ghosts could be so adorable," he replied.

"Technically, she isn't a ghost," I corrected. "She's a spirit. Ghosts are the shadows of beings that haven't passed through the light and onto the other side. Like the Native American at Puvungna."

"But you called him a spirit," Blue said, wrinkling his brow.

"They're all spirits," I explained. "In fact, in essence, you, me and Julie are spirits, we're just inside of a corporeal form for the time being."

"So ghosts are our spirits after we die, but before we move on to heaven?" he asked.

"Sure," I replied. "That's a good enough explanation for it. There's more to it than that, but let's not complicate things."

I was amazed that, for someone who had labeled himself as an authentic shaman, had taken the time to learn about the rhythms that ghosts prefer most, who had felt their energy and had so easily stirred them up, had so little understanding of them. Where I'd been skeptical of Blue before, I'd started to develop a new appreciation for him. The kid really wanted to learn and was open to the world. He'd just started into it the wrong way and gotten caught up in something that got out of control for him. Julie and I had come into his life at a critical time and for a very important reason.

"Where'd Mack go?" Blue asked, suddenly realizing that Mack was no longer sitting across from him. Evidently, he hadn't heard what Mack said before excusing himself from the table.

"He went to get Queenie," Julie replied.

"I'm going to take a guess," Blue grinned. "Queenie is another ghost? Or is she a spirit?"

"She's a ghost," I replied.

"Aren't we going to call her here too?"

"Normally we'd have to, but I have Mack."

"Mack brings ghosts to us," Julie pointed out.

"Sort of like a ghostly butler," Blue laughed.

"Please don't let him hear you say that," I warned.

"Who hear who say what?" Mack asked as he passed through the door.

"Nothing," I replied. I changed the subject. "You couldn't find her?"

"I found her," he replied. "She wasn't eager to come."

"Where is she?"

"She's outside. She's accustomed to the old

ways. She wants a formal invitation from the mistress of the house," he replied. His manner almost made me giggle, especially after Blue's earlier comment.

I closed my eyes, focused my energy to connect with that of the spirit of Queenie and extended a formal welcome to her. Within moments, the broken down form of a slight, Native American ghost came through the door. She said nothing. Her dark eyes scanned the room and she glared into the eyes of each of us for a very long moment.

"What do you want?" her raspy voice said after she was satisfied that she had given each of us a good going over.

"Welcome, Queenie, to my home."

"This otter said it was his home," she waved a hand toward Mack.

"We share it," I replied.

She glared at me for several seconds as she tried to make sense of how a corporal woman and ghost man shared a home.

"I'd like to introduce everyone, but they can't see you." I indicated Blue and Julie.

"Humph," she replied.

"I'll show you how," I said, extending the remote toward her.

"What is this?"

"It's something from which you can draw

energy in order to reveal yourself."

She examined the remote, not realizing that she had become visible to Julie and Blue. I started to reach for the remote, but she drew it back from me and scowled at me. She started to move her finger over the buttons. In the process, she unmuted the TV.

"What's that noise?" she asked, jumping back with a start. She noticed the TV and moved toward it.

"You've never seen a TV before?" I asked, a little surprised.

"How did they trap those people in that box?" She looked around behind the flat-screen TV and then frowned at me. "How do you make them stop talking?"

"With that." I motioned toward the remote.

"Here," she said, pushing it toward me. "Make them stop."

With the TV muted again, I started the introductions.

"Queenie, this is Blue and this is Julie."

She nodded toward each one of them in turn, but said nothing. She just stared at them for a very long time.

"You live here with the otter?" she grumbled, continuing to look around.

"I live here with Mack," I replied, indicating Mack.

"I call him the otter," she responded.

"Why do you call me that?" Mack asked.

"Because you call me Queenie," she replied.

"Isn't that your name?" Julie asked.

The woman stared at Julie for several ticks of the pendulum on the parlor clock.

"No, I just made up that name to get that little girl, Carla to leave me alone."

"So, your name isn't Queenie?" I asked. I sent a worried glance in the direction of Julie. Had we failed again?

"What is your name, then?" I asked.

"You too?" she groused.

I shrugged. "We could continue to call you Queenie."

"My name is Toypurina," she said.

Blue sucked in a sharp breath and then stared at her in much the same way that she'd stared at him earlier.

We all turned to look at Blue.

"What's the matter, did you see a ghost?" she quipped without cracking a smile.

"My grandfather told me about you," Blue whispered.

"I doubt I knew your grandfather," she growled. "I've been dead for more than two hundred years."

Chapter Eighteen

It took all of us, but Blue, several seconds to digest the number that Toypurina had just given us. Two hundred years was pretty hard to swallow.

"Never seen anyone so old before, huh?" she snorted. "The Sunset Tree is older than I am."

"My grandfather told me that you led a rebellion against the Mission San Gabriel Arcángel in 1785," Blue said. "It didn't turn out too well and you were brought to trial and found guilty of leading the revolt. You asked to be baptized and took on the Christian name of Regina. That's a Spanish form of 'queen.' You married a man, had three children and lived in Monterey until you died in 1799."

"Who was your grandfather?" she grumbled.

"My grandfather was called Anacapa. He was a proud healer of the Chumash."

"Chumash," she scoffed. She glared at him for another long, silent moment. "He told you all that?"

"Yes."

"And you remembered it?"

"Yes."

A smile started to form at the corner of her lips, but she forced it away. "I still don't like you. You look more like the clear eyes that have ruined this land. I thought I hated the Spaniards. I was thrilled when I saw the clear eyes drive them out and take lands from them that had been taken from us. I laughed until I saw what the clear eyes did to the land."

"Grandmother," Blue said. "How could you have seen the clear eyes come to the land? There were no clear eyes here until 1848."

"Grandmother?" She raised a single eyebrow. "At least you were taught manners. I was here, in this form and I was watching them. I watched the Spaniards continue to abuse my people and our lands and I watched them fall. I watched the clear eyes drive them out and then I watched our land be laid waste and saw it transformed into the ugliness that it is now."

From that point on, Toypurina began to lay out her story without anyone asking or prompting her to. Evidently, sitting on something that irritated you for two hundred years made you want to talk.

"I was the age of that little girl Carla when the Spaniards built the missions. At first, it was exciting. They were strange to us and their ways were exotic. What they said about their God and what they taught about this Jesus was appealing to many, but what came from their mouths and what they did with their hands were two different things. While they spoke of peace and love, they destroyed the land that we loved. While they spoke of peace and love, they would not honor the sacred ground where we had laid to rest those who we had loved. While they spoke of peace and love, they forbade us from holding our dances. They were brutal with women and children. Their cattle destroyed the meadows and defiled the streams where we drew our water. The Spaniards were trespassers and liars, whose hands did not follow behind their words.

"I was happy to watch the Spaniards as the clear eyes came in and began to drive them out. I laughed when they were forced to endure the loss of their land and the destruction of their ways. I laughed until the clear eyes began to make the Spanish pueblo larger. I haven't laughed in a very long time.

"They began to dig channels and force the rivers to go where they wanted them to go rather than where they were designed to go by the creator. They made streets and built houses, but they never stopped. They built more streets, they moved the rivers again. They built bigger houses and bigger buildings. They became like moss that eats up an entire pond, killing every living thing within it until there was nothing left.

"When they saw that nothing was left, they cleared out small places where they could plant trees and grass that didn't belong here."

She was starting to fade out, so I handed her the remote. She eyed me suspiciously, took it, and then continued talking.

"The clear eyes brought in strange things, just like this and that." She raised up the remote in her hand and motioned toward the TV with her lips. She glared at Blue. "I hated the Spaniards, but I have grown to hate the clear eyes more. I would pity you most of all, young man, if I could feel pity. You have a grandfather who was of the Chumash people, our neighbors, but you also have the look of the clear eyes. I don't doubt that one of your hearts lies to the other."

She finished speaking, but did not stop glaring at Blue. I waited for a few moments and then decided to intervene. I was curious as to why she hadn't gone on to the light. Two hundred years as a ghost was a very long time. I doubted that I could move her on to the light. Her time had come and gone, but that did not stop me from asking.

"Why did you not go to the light?" I asked.

"The light never came," she replied, turning her glare upon me.

"But you were baptized, married, had a family after the rebellion. Surely your life had become better."

"Baptism," she scoffed. "I only did that because if I hadn't, they would have sent me away to Mission San Carlos Borromeo de Carmelo, which was the farthest mission away from where I was born. In the end, it didn't matter. They sent me there anyway. It wasn't until I was dead that I returned to my home. I have stayed near the juniper tree since that time. It is the same one that was little more than a bush when I was a little girl. I nurture that tree and I've frightened away everyone who has tried to cut it out or harm it. It is dying. Soon, there will be nothing left of my home and I will wander. I do not know where I will go."

My heart ached for her. I couldn't imagine the depths of pain and bitterness in her. I couldn't conceive of how heavy it weighed on her, even as a ghost. Was there a way out for her? There had been a way for Carla's killer, who had never been offered the light. Was there some duty, something that Toypurina could do that would set things right for her?

Is she the queen that Ahau spoke of? Mack asked in my mind, having read my thoughts.

I don't know, maybe?

Then maybe if she helps us?

I suddenly saw a glimmer of hope.

Chapter Nineteen

"What can you and the otter do for me?" Toypurina scoffed. "I've been dead more than two hundred years and the light is not coming for me. There is no other chance for me."

Butting heads with Toypurina didn't seem like a good idea. I wasn't afraid of her. She growled, grumbled and glared, but I sensed that those things were covering up something else inside of her. She was angry and bitter because she had watched something that she loved be destroyed. Remembering how she had repeated the phrase "peace and love" earlier, I decided to try something different and hope it worked.

"What was it like here when you were a little girl?" I asked.

"Humph," she grunted. "It was beautiful.

Not like it is now."

"I'm amazed that the juniper tree, which was beside your home when you were a little girl, is still there. I didn't know that juniper trees lived that long."

"It would reach three times that age if there wasn't so much poison in the air and the water," she grumbled.

I wasn't getting anywhere and I was starting to become frustrated with our progress. Had we screwed up all around? We thought that we'd found the queen that Ahau had referred to, but maybe we had gotten completely off base. *I suppose you should just take her back to where she came from, Mack.*

I just finished the thought when a small, bright, light began to form above the table where we'd had the séance earlier. The light continued to grow and take on the shape of a person. The person was familiar to me and yet, not familiar.

"Ahau?" Julie asked. Something inside of her had instantly recognized the angel while I was still struggling with it.

"Julie," she replied. "I've missed you."

"I've missed you too."

The two of them embraced while I looked on in stunned silence. Julie had nourished a gift that I hadn't noticed in her before. I'd known she was an empath, but she had reached a level I'd not known about.

You might raise up your lower jaw, dahling.

"I see you've found the queen," the older Ahau said, turning toward me.

"I, uh, didn't recognize you, Ahau," I said. It was the only thing that I could get to come out of my mouth after taking Mack's advice and closing it.

"We angels come in different forms, depending upon our purpose, of course."

"You were a little girl before."

"The least frightening and intimidating form that can be taken on, don't you agree?"

Remembering the adorable little girl, I smiled. "I agree. What is your purpose now? We really don't know how to proceed from this point forward."

"The queen does," she said, turning toward Toypurina.

"I am not the queen, Queenie or Regina. I am Toypurina and my people are the Tongva."

I understood immediately why Ahau's child form wouldn't have worked. The angel stood her ground with great confidence. "When you were baptized, you took on the name of Regina. So, where heaven is concerned, that is your name."

"That is not the name in my heart,"

Toypurina snapped.

"No, it's not. In your heart, you are Toypurina. Your baptism was a lie and that is why you've been bound to the earth for 217 years." She glared at Toypurina with an intensity that I had never seen in any being before. "Would you like to walk into the light and join your ancestors, your children, your grandchildren and even your grandchildren's grandchildren? Or would you prefer to wander?"

"No light will come for me," Toypurina murmured.

"The light will come for you, but only after you complete a task."

"What task would that be?" the old ghost growled.

"Help restore order out of chaos," Ahau responded.

"I have no power to restore order out of chaos," Toypurina grumbled.

"Alone, you do not, but together with these," Ahau said, waving a hand around the room indicating each of us, "and with someone that you knew in your youth but neglected."

"I knew no one in my youth," Toypurina objected.

"Your bitterness has blocked her from your memory, then?" Ahau wasn't nearly as sweet as your stereotypical angel. In fact, she was a little bit frightening. "Don't tell me that you've forgotten Kuruvungna Spring and the mother of the land."

"There is no land left. What the Spaniards didn't destroy, the clear eyes destroyed. The mother of the land no longer exists. She died along with the land." I noticed tears welling up in Toypurina's eyes. In those tears were the source of her anger and bitterness. In those tears was her love of the land which had been taken from her and from her people.

"That is where you are wrong."

"I am not wrong," Toypurina snapped.

"Do you remember the story of Weywot's tyranny?"

"Of course I do. It is the story of our people."

"It is part of the story of your people. It is not the whole story."

"Grandmother," Blue interjected. "Tell us of Weywot's tyranny."

We all turned to look at Blue. He was pleading with her as though he knew that she had to remember the story and remember the love of her youth. His timing had been perfect and the way he had asked made it impossible for Toypurina to resist the telling. I was shocked. I had misjudged him badly. He truly had a heart for his grandfather's people. *Does*

Blue have a gift?
So it might seem, dahling.

"Weywot was the first ruler of all people. He was present as one of the creators of the land. Along with Quaoar, they created the mother of the land, Chehooit. Chehooit had brought blessing upon the land. She brought rich herbs, plants, trees and flowers. She provided the people with food to eat, provided the wild animals with food as well and provided medicines for the people."

Toypurina's eyes misted over as she spoke and the tears spilled over the rims and ran down her cheeks.

"Chehooit nourished the people even while Weywot was cruel to them. Weywot was tyrannical and heavy handed. His demands upon the people were too much for them to bear. Even the sons of Weywot felt his heavy weight upon their shoulders. Groaning from beatings that they'd received from their father, the sons of Weywot came to Chehooit and begged her to let them have some of the deadly plants that she guarded from the people.

"Feeling compassion for the sons of Weywot, Chehooit prepared a meal from the deadly plants and the boys took it home and presented it to their father. Weywot ate the meal that had been prepared for him and died. There was confusion after he died. There was chaos among the people. The sons of Weywot returned to Chehooit once more and asked for her help. Chehooit caused the land to cry out. The rocks, the trees, the waters, the grasses, the herbs... all living things cried out. Hearing the cries of the land, Quaoar came to the land and he began to teach the people. As he taught them the proper ways to live within the land, order was restored to the land."

"Toypurina," Ahau said in a softer tone. "Weywot has been awaked from his sleep and chaos has come to the land again. If you will help restore order, then you can join your people." The moment she finished speaking, Ahau vanished.

CHANEL SMITH

Chapter Twenty

Mack, Julie, Blue and I sat in stunned silence as we watched the hardened Toypurina sobbing before us. She kept her head covered with her hands and her body shook as two hundred years of anguish poured out from her. As the burdensome moans began to lessen, Blue leaned forward and reached out toward her with a trembling hand.

"Grandmother," he said. "I must confess something to you."

"What must you confess?" she moaned.

"I must confess that the chaos that has brought Weywot back is because of me."

The old woman's head snapped up and she glared at him. "You awakened Weywot? How do you know it?"

"We have seen him," I replied. Though it was Blue's fault, I couldn't allow him to face her by himself. I hadn't known who the powerful spirit that we'd faced at Puvungna had been until I'd heard what Ahau had said and had begun to put it all together.

Wow! No wonder he was so powerful. He's a god.

We're lucky to have escaped.

Toypurina didn't turn to look at me. She kept her glare focused on Blue. "Do you know what you've done? The Spaniards brought chaos to the land and on its heels the clear eyes, but neither of these know the cruelty of Weywot. How have you done this thing? Why have you done it? Do not let one of your hearts lie to the other any longer. Tell me the truth with both of your hearts."

Toypurina listened quietly, though I could see the wrath building up in her eyes and knew that once Blue finished the telling how he had awakened Weywot that the old woman was going to unleash upon him with great fury. In that moment, I saw myself. I saw how I had been angry at Blue and had judged him for having been irresponsible. I also saw what might have been if I had allowed that anger to take root. By chance, I looked up at Julie. I saw in her eyes and felt in her presence the same thoughts. She hadn't been angry at Blue. Her anger had been toward me. She moved her lips giving me a silent, "I'm sorry" and I responded with, "Me too."

Just as I had guessed, when Blue had finished telling how his drumming had awakened Weywot and what had been the result, Toypurina laid into him.

"You used a sacred ceremony to make money? It is a heresy! Why were you not warned after the first time? Do you not understand that the rattlesnakes were a warning to you?"

"I do now," he mumbled, studying his feet.

"You of the two hearts. With one heart, you drum out the ceremonial rhythms of your people and with the other you make yourself rich. Did not your Chumash heart speak truth to your clear eyed heart?"

"It did," he admitted. "But I did not listen."

"It is a foolish and irresponsible thing that you've done. Weywot is not someone to be played with like a child's toy or a kitten's ball of string."

I felt my anger beginning to rise up inside of me. Blue deserved part of what he was getting, but Toypurina was about to go too far. I could sense it. By the look on Julie's face, she could sense it too.

"I want to help make it right," Blue pleaded. "That's why I came to Pauline, Julie and Mack."

"You'll be nowhere near me when I go to make this right!" she roared. "I don't need your lying hearts…"

"That's enough!" Julie bellowed, rising up from her seat and leaning to within inches of Toypurina's face. "What Blue did was wrong. He's acknowledged that many times. He has taken every step right along with us to help fix this problem and he's going to continue taking steps along with us. So get that through your bitter old soul. Dig up the compassion of your youth that Ahau was talking about. You harped upon how the Spaniards spoke of peace and love while they destroyed the land. You destroy without speaking of peace and love. Maybe Blue has two hearts, but both of them are good hearts. They're nothing like the one bitter, black one that you have."

Silence reigned after Julie finished. Toypurina looked away from everyone and sighed heavily.

"We have a problem to solve tomorrow," I said in a quiet voice. "We're going to solve it together and when we do, you can walk through the light to join your people. Will you come with us to Kuruvungna Springs tomorrow?"

"I will come," she whispered.

"Are you two coming?" I asked Blue and Julie.

"Yes," they replied.

"Do any of you know how to get there?" I asked.

"I do," Blue answered.

"Okay, then, here is the plan. Mack will go get Toypurina when we wake up and bring her back here. We'll all go to Kuruvungna Springs in the morning and do whatever it is we need to do there. Do you know what we need to do, Toypurina?"

"We need to call up Chehooit," she replied.

"Can I do that as a medium?"

"No."

"How do we do it then?"

"With drums."

"Then we need Blue, don't we?" I was trying to remain calm. Her anger had made her irrational and she had been working against herself.

"Yes."

"Well, then, we'll all go our separate ways for the evening, cool off and then start fresh tomorrow. How's that sound?"

Take her home, Mack.

"Come on Toypurina," Mack said. "I'll take you back to the juniper tree. With any luck, this will be the last night you have to sleep under it."

Toypurina looked up at him with a mixture of emotions that were so muddled that they were hard to read and then followed him through the door.

"Wow!" I sighed heavily when they were gone. "That got pretty intense."

"You're telling me," Julie responded.

"She was right, though," Blue said. "What I did was irresponsible."

"The important thing, though, babe," Julie answered, no longer worried about how she addressed him, "is that you're trying to make it right. All too often, people want forgiveness without repenting and trying to set things right first."

Blue shrugged.

"Let's go home," Julie said, taking him by the hand. "What time tomorrow, Pauline?"

I looked at the clock. "Wow, 11:00 is going to come early, but that's probably when we need to start."

"11:00 it is," Julie said, leaning in to give me a kiss on the cheek before she led Blue out the door.

Chapter Twenty-one

I was finishing off my second cup of coffee, and had read the black and white funnies and the obits, when I heard Julie's special knock on the door and then her call as she pushed the door open.

Just like old times.

Mack smiled at me as I passed along the thought. *Time for me to go, then.*

We'd already decided that Julie and Blue's arrival would be his signal that it was time to go get Toypurina. As he left, I went to greet Julie and Blue. It felt so good to hug and kiss her, just like we'd always done when before whenever we greeted one another. Offering the same greeting to Blue was a wonderful addition and it felt very natural; like he was a part of our oddly-assembled family.

"How you feeling?" Blue asked. He hadn't forgotten that I'd been zapped by Weywot and knocked unconscious the day before.

"I could have slept a couple more hours, but I'm fine," I replied. Though I felt some trepidation, I was eager to get going and get our problem—and L.A.'s problem—solved. "Besides, most of it's on you today."

"Don't I know it," Blue sighed. He raised his eyebrows, which had the effect of widening his incredibly pale, blue eyes.

"Clear eyes," I laughed.

Julie and Blue wrinkled their brows and posed their unspoken question.

"Your eyes," I glanced over at Julie as well. Hers had more a green hue to them, but they were just as pale and clear. "Both of you. I know why they called us Anglos clear eyes. It makes total sense."

Julie put a hand on my forehead and laughed. "You're sure you're okay?"

"What's the plan, boss?" Blue asked. I could tell by the way he fiddled with his fingers that he was anxious to get down to business.

There really wasn't any point in keeping him waiting. "Mack has gone to get Toypurina. We'll leave as soon as she gets back. Unless her demeanor has improved a great deal, and I have my doubts, the less time we have to spend sitting around with her, the better. Am I right?"

"Totally," Blue agreed. "My heart aches for her. Both of them do. Her bitterness must be terribly heavy and must cause her so much pain."

It seemed that Blue had turned what Toypurina had meant as derogatory into a positive attribute. It was a good indicator of the depth of his character; a very good sign. "Then lead her to her rest, Blue," I responded. During the night, his purpose had become clear to me and I had hoped for an opportunity to communicate that to him. I was happy that it came so easily. It didn't usually happen that way.

Blue smiled and nodded, and then his expression turned serious again. "So, we're all riding together to Kuruvungna?"

"Heavens no! I would never put a bunny in a cage with a wildcat," I laughed. "You might be her salvation, but she probably won't embrace you; maybe not until the very end and maybe never."

"It doesn't matter if she does or not," he replied. "But you're right, the least amount of time I am around her, the better off it is for all of us."

"I'd send you two on your way ahead of us, if I didn't need to follow you in order to find the place."

"We could wait in the car," Julie suggested. "Avoid an encounter altogether, at least until we get to the spring."

"Great idea," I agreed.

Except we're heah. Mack's voice responded inside my head. A fraction of a second later, he and Toypurina came through the door and into the front room.

"They're here, aren't they?" Julie observed.

"They are," I said. "You two go on out to the car. We're right behind you."

Toypurina glared at Blue, but said nothing. Fortunately for Blue, he couldn't see her, even though he nearly walked through her on his way to the door.

"Are you ready, Toypurina?" I smiled, hoping that a little bit of a good mood would rub off on her.

"Might as well," she said. "Where are those clear eyes going? I thought they were coming with us."

"They're going in a different car," I responded.

"Is that one of those horseless wagons that I see the clear eyes riding in all the time?"

"Yes."

"Noisy, dirty, disgusting things," she spat. "And there are millions of them adding their poison to the air. That's probably what's killing my juniper tree."

I could argue against her point, but neither could I change the culture that we lived in. Instead of making an attempt argue or agree, I decided to just get going. "We need to get started. We have a long day ahead of us."

"You and the other two go on. Me and the otter will catch up with you."

I looked up and smiled. *Hey, at least otters are cute.*

Gee, how wondahful, he drawled in my mind.

I was sure that I was going to have another challenge on my hands when it came time to get her in the car, but Mack and I had already discussed it over coffee that morning. Kicking and screaming, if necessary, she was going into the car.

When we arrived out in the parking lot in front of the apartment building, I noticed that Blue and Julie were already in the Spider, which they had pulled out of its parking place, and were waiting for us. I went directly to the driver's side, opened the door and got in. "Get in."

"We're going to ride in that thing?" Toypurina asked.

"Yes," I responded.

"You ride in those things, Otter?" she asked, looking up at Mack, who dwarfed her with his size.

"All the time," Mack replied.

I was expecting an outburst that would be followed by a struggle as Mack hauled her kicking and screaming into the back seat of the car. It didn't come.

"Hmmm," she responded as she timidly moved through the door into the back seat. Her eyes inspected every inch of the interior of my car, much like they had inspected my home the night before.

I turned the ignition and started the motor.

"What's that?" she asked with wide eyes.

"That the engine," I answered. "It's what makes the car go, since we don't have horses."

"That's what makes the foul smoke in the air too," she groused.

I ignored her comment and we started on her way. Much to my surprise, Toypurina settled into the back seat of the car and remained quiet as I followed along behind Blue in the Spider. We arrived at the site of Kuruvungna Springs and Mack let out a loud exclamation just as I pulled into the parking lot, causing me to slam on my brakes as my head attempted to shoot through the roof of the car.

"Kuruvungna!"

"Mack!" I should have expected it, really.

"I like that one better than Puvungna," he grinned.

I looked over my shoulder just in time to see Toypurina stop laughing. The sour expression returned to her face. "I like this otter."

She likes me.

Showers of blessings, I replied, though I could recall the rest of the song.

Mack laughed at me. I parked the car and we got out and moved toward where Blue and Julie were waiting.

Blue stepped forward as we approached. He could see neither Mack nor Toypurina, but that did not stop him from greeting them. "Grandmother, I hope you are well today."

"Hrumf," she grunted.

"She says that she is well," I replied.

"I said nothing of the sort," she replied.

"Shall we?" I said, ignoring her again.

CHANEL SMITH

Chapter Twenty-two

Blue proved to be a greater asset than we'd first realized. Visitors were not allowed into the fenced off area of Kuruvungna Spring except for on the first Saturday of each month. Blue, however, because of his tribal credentials, was able to enter the area and bring Julie and I with him.

Kuruvungna, in contrast to Puvungna, was alive and thriving. It was well marked. Its pools were kept clean, in some cases enclosed by stone. There was an abundance of flora and fauna all around the springs. There were birds, butterflies and bees about; chirping, flitting and buzzing, according to their vocations. I glanced at Toypurina as we moved forward and watched the most amazing transformation begin to spread over her face. I had been right about her. Her anger and bitterness had been a cover for the love of nature that was in her heart. The proof was unveiling itself right before my eyes.

"You see, Grandmother," Blue commented. "The land is not dead. It lives still."

She frowned at him, but did not respond.

Blue continued forward, not looking for or expecting a response. He too, I noticed, was lost in the life that surrounded him.

They're alike! Mack's thought came into my head, stealing the one that I was about to form.

It didn't matter. I smiled at him. I loved the fact that we shared the space inside my mind in moments like that.

We strolled about a few moments soaking in the tranquility of Kuruvungna and the escape that it provided from the clambering city that surrounded us. It was a sanctuary, like that of any grand cathedral, a place of escape, of renewal and of transformation. However, unlike the stone walls, it was alive with hope, promise and new life. My spirit was being drawn in and it began to soar along with the birds.

"Shall we get started?" Blue said in a reverent tone.

I could see the fear in his eyes. He knew what he was doing. He was very aware of the effect that it would have and he was not going into the drumming lightly. I smiled at him, as Julie stepped forward and took his hand in hers.

"Let's do it," Julie whispered.

Blue lowered his pack and produced three drums. "I wish I had two more, but I..."

"Not a problem, Blue," I smiled. "They understand."

"I could drum," Mack protested. "I could go get a charge from the battery on that Spider and drum all day long."

Mack!

Blue started off with a beat that Julie and I repeated. We practiced several times where we stood, until Julie and I had picked up on the correct rhythm and then we began to follow the paths around the pools and through the brush and trees, continuing to drum.

I watched Toypurina and Mack, not surprised that Toypurina had closed her eyes and was swaying to the rhythm, but shocked that Mack was doing the same. Evidently, the spirits were entranced and stirred by that beat. As I was watching them, I was startled by a low moaning sound that began to rise from Toypurina's chest. It grew in volume and then became like a song and chant combined into one. Though I could not understand the words, I could feel the deep emotion that was in them. I could see the tears streaming down her face as she turned her face skyward and continued her song.

Just like I'd seen happen with Ahau, a tiny bright light began to form among us. Just as with Ahau, the light grew larger and brighter and then began to take shape.

"Chehooit," Blue whispered.

Chehooit ignored him. She ignored all of us, focusing her gentle gaze upon Toypurina. "My daughter," she said. "Why do you wail? Why do you sing this song of sadness in this place of life?"

Toypurina turned her face toward Chehooit. "For the land, holy one," she responded. "For the destruction and chaos that is all around us."

"You must stop, my daughter. The land is not destroyed. There is order."

"There cannot be order, holy one," Toypurina whispered in a reverent tone. "Weywot has been awakened."

"Weywot has been awakened?" A troubled look came onto the face of Chehooit, replacing that which had been brilliant with eternal hope. "How is this so?"

Blue started to step forward, but I held up a hand, signaling him to stop. I wanted to see how Toypurina was going to respond.

Toypurina looked toward Blue. For an instant, I saw her consider placing the blame upon him, but in its place came something different. She looked back at Chehooit and responded. "It matters not how. It only matters that order is restored. These spirits," she said, waving her hand in a sweeping circle that included Blue, Julie, Mack and me, "have all come in order to help order to be restored."

"Who are these blessed spirits?" Chehooit asked.

Toypurina began with me and introduced us in turn around the circle coming to Mack last. "Pauline, Julie, Blue and..." To my shock, she started to giggle as she came to Mack. "The Otter."

Blue, Julie, Mack and I all exchanged startled glances at the sound of laughter coming from the cranky old hag who had barely cracked a smile in our presence before that moment. I was even more shocked that Mack accepted his name, almost as if he was proud to be introduced that way.

No complaints?

I looked it up. An otter is greatly honored among the Natives.

Chehooit's head moved from me to Mack and back again as she picked up our conversation. She picked up a great deal more than that, based on the knowing smile.

"Where is Weywot?" Chehooit asked.

"Puvungna," I answered.

"We must go there at once."

"It will take us some time," I responded. "We must travel on the earth."

"Of course," Chehooit chuckled. "Call me when you arrive."

"How do we call you?" I asked.

"Blue knows," she replied and then vanished.

Chapter Twenty-three

We approached Puvungna with a great deal of caution. I led off with Mack and Toypurina flanking me. After the experience with Weywot before, I was none too eager to stumble upon the powerful spirit and be surprised by him.

As we crept forward, I tried to keep my senses open and in tune for the energies that would surely be in the area. To my surprise, I felt nothing. I was confused.

"Mack?" I didn't have to say more. I knew he was reading my thoughts.

"I'm not picking up anything either."

Toypurina remained silent. She no longer had the fixed scowl on her face that she'd had before. In place of it was a determined, focused expression. I wondered if that was how she had appeared when she'd led the rebellion against the Spanish mission. No doubt, she had been a very influential person among her people.

When we were within the grove of trees, I paused, and then strolled in a full circle, still not picking up any energy. I glanced over at Blue, knowing that he would have to lead us in drumming in order to call Chehooit, but also knowing that he would be calling up Weywot at the same time.

Blue closed his eyes, inhaled and exhaled heavily, and then placed his pack on the ground. The fear that was in his eyes at Kuruvungna was nothing compared to what was in them as he took out the drums and passed two of them to Julie and me.

"Ready," he said, just above a whisper.

Julie and I nodded.

Blue started out with his first beats and Julie and I repeated them. Much sooner than we had at Kuruvungna, we were drumming in unison and winding our way among the trees of the grove. Mack and Toypurina, just as they had done before, were swaying rhythmically to the beat. When Toypurina began her song at Puvungna, it was entirely different. Instead of being filled with mournful wails, there was more of a menacing tone to the words. The emotions were not emotions of anguish, but of resolution, discipline and authority.

I felt the same powerful and sinister presence that I'd felt at Briar Summit beginning to flow around us. After some moments, I began to see the faces of the warrior spirits, just as I'd seen at Briar Summit, and then those faces began to transform into the faces of ravens, bears, wolves and cougars. Each of those faces cried out, seeming to increase in power because of our fear. A bright light came up in the center of the circle of fierce animals. The light surrounding the figure was not brilliant and pure in the same way that Ahau and Chehooit had done, but it arose in a similar fashion. When the form took shape, it was Weywot.

Blue stopped drumming and stood dumbfounded as he looked around him. I could tell that, by some odd phenomenon that he and Julie could see all of the spirits. The horror in their eyes, without a doubt, was exactly the same as was in mine. We had called up Weywot, but we had not called up Chehooit.

What do we do now? It was the shared question of Mack and me.

"You have returned with the heretic, then?" Weywot laughed.

The warriors, in the forms of the fierce animals surrounding us, were poised to strike at any moment. They needed only the command of

Weywot to release them.

"Weywot!" Toypurina's voice called out in a tone of authority. "You are not welcome among the people. You and your minions must return to your place among the dead."

"Not without the heretic's blood!"

"You have no claim on the heretic's blood. Only the people have that claim."

"The people are weak. They need discipline to return them to their strength."

"We are stronger than you know," Toypurina responded.

I had watched the anger building in his eyes as Toypurina issued her challenge and I knew that he was about to strike. I was right.

"Let me test your strength!" he bellowed as a powerful force of energy, exactly like the one he'd used to strike me, was hurtled toward Toypurina.

In the very same instant the stream of energy left him, I saw Blue leap in front of Toypurina. The force of the stream hit him full in the chest and he tumbled backward. Julie, who had anticipated what he was doing, was already in motion toward him. Being caught off-guard by Blue's movement, I was still frozen in place.

The stream of energy also released the waiting warriors, who rushed toward us. Fearing that Julie, Blue or both would be possessed just like Amanda had, I rushed toward them. I had no concept of what I would be able to do for them, but I couldn't allow it to happen. I saw a wolf hovering over Blue, who had collapsed, unconscious on the ground. Julie was on her knees beside him and calling to him. A bear was poised to leap upon her.

As I rushed forward, I was intercepted by a cougar crouched in front of me while a raven was circling around me and diving at my head. In the very moment that I was certain that all was lost, three, brilliant balls of light rose up out of Blue, Julie and Toypurina. Each of them grew in size and took on a new form, casting off the snarling creatures that were hovering over Blue and Julie.

When fully formed, the three of them stood shoulder to shoulder, forming an impenetrable wall in front of Julie, Blue and Toypurina. Their eyes held a menacing glare, which made the fierce animals cower and shrink away from them. They gathered behind Weywot, but held little of the fierceness they'd had before.

Two of the glowing forms I recognized as the forms of Ahau and Chehooit, but I did not know the third. I glanced at Mack, whose mouth was open in an expression of shock.

You'll want to raise your lowah jaw, dahling, I mocked, not sure how I had suddenly been able to regain my humor in such a grave moment.

"Weywot!" Chehooit bellowed with a voice of authority that did not match her feminine form. "You are not welcome among the people!"

"I was called to be among the people by the heretic!" he objected forcefully, pointing a long, bony finger at Blue. "Give me his blood and I will return."

I noticed that Blue had recovered from the blow and was being helped to his feet by Julie. The same blow had knocked me out for close to an hour. I figured it had something to do with the force of energy that had come up out of him. In fact, it had probably been that same energy that had made it so that he could see the spirits. As he stood, his eyes were fixed upon the third angel that I did not recognize. He stared at him and would not avert his gaze.

"How you were called here or by whom does not matter!" Chehooit responded. "You were banished to the place of the dead and you will return there! Without his blood."

"By what authority?"

Chapter Twenty-four

With the force of fierce creatures, who had suddenly regained their ferocity, snarling and snapping behind Weywot, who stood in defiance against the three angels. It looked like a stalemate to me. Weywot had made his claim upon the blood and issued his challenge against the authority of the three angels. There was a long moment of silence latent with forces of energy that so were so extreme that I could feel their weight pressing against my chest, making it difficult to breathe.

And then something extraordinary began to happen. The brilliant light of the three angels began to merge into an enormous ball of energy. At the same instant that the three forms were merging together inside of the ball, another, much larger, form began to take shape. The shape continued to rise until it was more than twice my height, broad and thick across his chest and with limbs that rivaled the largest branches of the surrounding trees.

"By the authority of Quaoar," the weighty, baritone voice responded.

Though his confidence was visibly rattled at the sight of Quaoar, Weywot remained defiant. "And if I refuse?"

"You will not refuse," Quaoar answered.

I guess I thought that Weywot was smarter than he was. I guess he was just one of those types who, even when he knew he was defeated, had to continue his defiance. I saw the energy beginning to build up inside of him and knew that he was preparing to give Quaoar everything he had. Instinctively, I crouched and covered my head and looked toward Quaoar, anticipating his response.

Quaoar's eyes twinkled in gleeful anticipation of Weywot's coming blow, but did not seem to be making any preparation to deliver one in return. I looked back toward Weywot in time to see him release a stream of energy, which had to have been three or four times more powerful than what he'd used on Blue and I. In response, Quaoar extended a massive hand, caught the full force of the stream and walked steadily toward Weywot, holding back and pressing the stream back toward where it was radiating from Weywot.

As Quaoar backed Weywot's stream back toward him, Weywot's strength began to fade. He slowly faded to his knees before Quaoar. As Weywot's power faltered, the fierce animals behind him cowered, shrunk to the ground and then became human forms once more. They cried out in agony along with their master, as the stream of energy was pressed closer and closer toward Weywot's chest. Then, they began to shrivel up into tiny streams, sort of like clouds and were being sucked back into Weywot's body.

Weywot's forehead fell to the ground in front of Quaoar and he began to plead with Quaoar. Great wailing and screeching sounds came from the once powerful spirit as Quaoar stood over him and continued to turn all of Weywot's energy back upon him. Weywot could no longer remain on his knees and collapsed to the ground, entirely prone at the feet of Quaoar as streams of clouds, just like the ones that I'd seen as the warriors were transformed, were drawn in from all around us, being sucked back into the body of Weywot.

Once the streams had all been drawn into his body, the screeching form of Weywot began to shrivel up as well. In the same instant that I saw his form be reduced to nothing, the massive, brilliant form of Quaoar vanished.

My breathing and the beating of my heart seemed much too loud in the moment of absolute stillness that surrounded us. I looked around and took in the remaining forms of Blue, Julie, Toypurina and Mack. No one could speak nor make any movement beyond glancing around at our odd assembly.

Surprisingly, it was Toypurina who moved first, striding slowly toward Blue, who could no longer see her. Julie, who could not see her either, felt Toypurina's presence as she moved toward Blue. Julie positioned herself next to him in a protective fashion.

It's okay, Jules. Wait a second.

She looked up at me and nodded a response.

Toypurina reached Blue and took hold of one of his hands. Instinctively, feeling the chilling touch, Blue jumped and drew back his hand.

"It's okay, Blue," I said. "It's Toypurina. She wants to hold your hand."

Toypurina turned to look at me. "He can't see me?"

"No."

"Can he hear me?" she asked.

"No."

"She wants to know if you can see or hear her," I told Blue as Mack and I moved nearer to them.

"Will this help?" Blue asked, drawing his cell phone out of his pocket and holding it up for me.

It was a pretty dim energy source, but it might be enough if Blue was extremely receptive to her energy. "You can give it a try."

Blue extended the cell phone in front of him.

"Take it," I said to Toypurina.

"What is it?" she asked.

"It's a cellular phone," I said.

The confused expression on her face told me that the concept was entirely alien to her.

"They're what we use now to make a phone call..." I stopped myself as it dawned on me that a telephone and a phone call would have no meaning for her either. "It's like the thing we had in my home."

"Don't we need the box with the people in it too?" she asked, looking around her.

I smiled. "No. It won't be very strong, but it will help."

Toypurina took the phone. I could tell that she had appeared before Blue by the reaction he and Julie made. Neither of them had expected her to be so close to them.

"I can see you, Grandmother," Blue said.

"Are you okay?"

"I am fine, Grandson," she replied. She extended her hand toward him. "Walk with me a moment, please."

The two turned and began to stroll into the grove of trees. Julie started to follow, but Toypurina stopped her with a raised hand. Julie looked at me. *What's she doing?*

Just trust her. Do you have your cell phone?

Julie pulled out her phone and showed it to me.

"Give it to Blue," I directed. I didn't know how long Toypurina could remain visible from the energy from Blue's cell phone.

"Blue," Julie called out, striding to catch up to the pair and extending the cell phone toward him.

Blue took it, grinning broadly as he and Toypurina strolled off into the trees.

Chapter Twenty-five

"Will the light come for her?" Julie asked as she moved over beside me.

"I have no way of knowing," I replied.

"She's changed dramatically," Julie smiled.

"We all have," I agreed, matching her expression.

"What do you suppose they're talking about?"

"I could guess, but I don't know."

"About the land, about his drumming, about the people? Those sorts of things?" Julie asked.

"Maybe. She might be apologizing to him for being so hard on him before."

"Like I should be doing to you," Julie said.

"I think I needed to change. You forced me to change."

"I didn't mean to force you."

"Okay, actually, you didn't force me, but our friendship forced me. I came to realize that I valued our friendship more than I valued those attitudes and things that I was holding onto. Holding onto those things so tightly was what was behind the way I was treating you. For that, I am truly, truly sorry."

"This whole thing." Julie waved a finger in the air, drawing a small circle that took in the area where the drama we'd witnessed had played out. "Reminded me of how much I missed being with you."

"This?" I laughed, repeating the same motion with my finger that she just had. I knew what she meant, but I was teasing her.

"You know what I mean. Not just this, but the whole thing. We belong together. We're a team."

"We do belong together," I responded.

With my focus on Blue and Toypurina, and then upon Julie, I hadn't felt Mack hovering by, not heard his thoughts being inserted into my head. I turned in a full circle, not seeing him.

"What's wrong?" Julie asked.

"Where's Mack?"

"I haven't seen him," she laughed.

I smirked at her. "He was right here with us when everything was over, but I have no idea when he left."

"Did you check Blue's car?"

I had to take several steps forward to see around some trees and get a decent view of the parking lot. I located Blue's car and also, sitting behind its steering wheel, I located Mack. He waved at me, beaming with delight.

"You nailed that one," I laughed. "He's sort of like a child."

"All men are," Julie laughed.

"Is Blue like that?" I said, narrowing my eyes and pushing my lips together into a knowing smile.

"I said, 'all men', didn't I?"

"So, what's up with you two?" I asked. "I don't mean to be nosy."

"Liar!" she screeched, smacking me on the shoulder. "You've been dying to get me alone so you could grill me for details."

I shrugged and broadened my grin.

Julie considered my question for a moment and had formed a response on her lips when Blue and Toypurina joined us. We turned toward them and the opportunity to hear what she had to say had been lost.

"Well?" Julie asked. "What have you two been talking about?"

"Deep secrets," Toypurina responded in a hushed tone. Her face had undergone a transformation that was so complete that I hardly recognized her. Her eyes were bright and the pain of bitterness that had kept her bent over was no longer there. She stood straight and walked like, like a queen.

"Yep, deep secrets," Blue agreed.

Toypurina patted his hand like a proud grandmother does when she holds her grandson's hand.

As I stood there admiring the changes that I could see in both of them, I could feel a soothing warmth begin to rise up behind me. It wasn't the first time I'd felt that warmth and I knew exactly what it was. Toypurina's light had come. Before turning around, I noticed Blue was peering over my shoulder.

"What's that?" he asked.

Julie and I turned to look in the direction he was looking. Before I could answer, Toypurina answered.

"My light," she smiled.

Just as she spoke, I could tell that she'd disappeared, because Blue began to panic.

"Did she already go? I can't see her. I didn't get to say goodbye."

Toypurina touched his hand again. Instead of jumping, Blue turned his face toward hers. His eyes were blind, but his heart was not.

"I'm still here, Grandson," she said.

I snatched my cell phone out of my pocket

and extended it to Toypurina. Toypurina accepted it from me without any questions.

"Can you see me now?" she asked.

"I can see you, Grandmother," Blue replied. "I know you must go into the light. I don't want you to stay in this world and wander, but I will miss you."

"You will never miss me," she replied. "When you hear the trickling of water in a stream, that will be my voice speaking to you. When a meadowlark is singing in the meadow, that will be my song of blessing for you. When the wind rustles the grass or stirs the leaves of the aspen tree, I'll be moving around you. When you smell the sweet fragrance of the cedar or drink cool water from a spring, that will be the scent of me and the taste of me. Do you understand, Grandson?"

"I understand, Grandmother," he replied.

"Good," she said. "Now, protect the land. Protect it with both of your hearts, for they are both strong. They are both full of love and peace."

"I will do as you say, Grandmother," Blue replied.

They embraced one last time, looked into each other's eyes for a lingering moment, and then Toypurina turned to Julie.

"You take good care of this young man. You

have a great heart and great gifts. With the force of your three hearts, you will be powerful."

"I will," Julie answered, embracing Toypurina and then wiping the tears from her eyes as the old woman turned away from her.

"Pauline," Toypurina continued. "Your gift is strong, but it is your heart that makes it so powerful. I can say little more than thank you, though there is a great deal more I wish that I could form into words."

"That," I said, motioning toward the light and the glowing form, which was waiting to lead her up the stairway, "is my reward."

She nodded and then wrinkled her brow. "Where's the otter?"

"Oh, he won't come near the light," I replied.

"Okay." She shrugged and wrapped me in a ghostly embrace, which I'd actually come to enjoy, because they were usually associated with the same moment we were experiencing. "Tell him goodbye for me."

She started toward the light, paused and turned back. "And he's right, you know. Otters are highly honored among my people."

Toypurina scanned our faces one last time, turned toward the light, took the hand of the attendant that was waiting for her and did not look back again as she started up the stairway.

Chapter Twenty six

"Dahling, did you find the sports page in the papah this morning?" Mack asked.

I had the paper spread out in front of me, had a full mug of steaming coffee sitting beside it and was chuckling softly as I read the black and white funnies. I looked up as he drew near and started ruffling the papers with his ghostly hand.

"Hey, what are you doing?"

"The sports page," he repeated.

"Hold on a second," I replied. "Let me look."

I flipped up the edges of the paper until I came to the sports section. I pulled that section out and handed it to him.

"Um hmmm," he murmured. "This always

happens when you get the papah instead of me."

"Oops. Sorry."

Mack settled in across the table with the sports section spread out in front of him. I finished the funnies and was still smiling from one of them as I flipped to the obits. The obits didn't mean much to a lot of people, but to me, they represented the spirits of people who were either moving into the light or who were struggling and might need my help. I had barely read the first one when I heard Julie's special knock on the front door and then her voice as she pushed the door open and called out.

"Back here in the kitchen, Jules!"

I looked up as she came through the front room and dining room of the open designed apartment. Before the two of them arrived in the kitchen, I could tell that they were about to make an enormous announcement. *They're engaged.*

Shush, Pauline. Let them tell us.

"Don't you look cozy, Pauline?" Julie said.

Mack rattled the edge of the sports section.

"Hi, Mack," Julie said.

"Hi, Mack," Blue repeated.

I reached for the remote, turned on the small TV in the kitchen, muted it and then slid the remote across the table to Mack. For what was about to come, it was better if Julie and Blue could see him.

"Don't the two of you look cozy?" Julie repeated her earlier phrase, adding emphasis to the slight change.

"Pull up a chair," I ordered, getting up, taking two mugs down from the cupboard and filling them with what was left in the pot. I placed the mugs in front of the two, who were grinning like they were up to something. "You know, my grandmother was from Georgia. She had the most peculiar saying for the sort of expression that the two of you have."

"Yeah, Pauline?" Blue asked. "What was that?"

"What has the two of you grinning like a possum eating shit with a hairbrush?"

"What?" Julie asked, bursting into a fit of uncontrollable laughter as she caught a visual image of the words.

Blue had raised his cup to his mouth for a sip of coffee and then brought it down hard as he had the same visualization. He splattered coffee all over the paper and nearly broke the mug in the process.

"Pauline!" Mack called out, bursting with laughter along with Julie and Blue.

Their laughter was so intense that, even though I'd heard it a thousand times, I couldn't help but join in. The visual image, just like it always did, popped up in my mind as well.

For several minutes, we eat took turns, mimicking what a possum engaged in such crude behavior might look like.

"Yep," I said, as Julie took her turn. "That's the exact look. So, what are the two of you up to?"

Their smiles didn't fade, but they looked across at each other, nodding an unspoken, "ready?" and then Julie drew her hand out of her pocket and displayed the ring on her finger.

"Blue and I are engaged," she gushed.

"Of course you are," I burst out. I'd known the minute they walked in and I'd been bursting to let it out too. I wrapped my arms around her and squeezed her as tight as I could.

While I was giving Julie the squeeze, Mack extended a ghostly fist toward Blue for a "paranormal fist bump," as the two had begun to call it. "That's great!"

We switched, with Mack giving Julie a ghostly embrace, which didn't make her nearly as uncomfortable as it once did, and I gave Blue a squeeze that was just as tight as the one I'd given Julie moments before.

"I know you're already sort of a part of our dysfunctional fraternity," I said, as I drew away and sat back down. "But I guess, now, it's official."

"Not quite official," he said. "We're not married yet."

"Technical," I laughed.

"What's wrong with technical?" Mack objected. "I like technical, don't you, Blue?"

Blue shrugged. "Sure."

"Hey!" Mack said. "Does this mean I get to drive your car?"

"Mack! You're a ghost for crying out loud."

"Hey, I do a lot of stuff. I get the papah. I change the channels. I buy stuff on the computer."

"None of those things are driving a car," I replied. "And thanks for reminding me that we need to have our talk about the credit card."

Mack made an expression like he was scared and then winked at me.

"Don't you wink at me, mister."

The conversation faltered for a moment and the three of us took a sip from our mugs in unison as we all eyed Mack.

"Kuruvungna!" Mack cried out, holding up an imaginary coffee mug in his hand before mimicking us and sending all of us into another fit of laughter.

As the laughter died down again, thoughts of what we had gone through together took over my mind. Specifically, there was a thought, an image really, that I'd forgotten about until that moment. That image was of the three angels that had suddenly risen up out of Julie, Blue and Toypurina. I remembered recognizing Chehooit and Ahau, but not the third angel. I also remembered that Blue had clearly recognized the third.

"Blue, I have a question for you," I began.

"Alright."

"You remember the three angels that rose up and stood in front of you, Julie and Toypurina, right?"

"Yep," he grinned, already knowing what I was about to ask him. He nodded and winked across the table at Julie. Evidently, he'd already shared his secret with her.

"I recognized Chehooit and Ahau, but I didn't know the third. You, however, very obviously did, so, who was the third angel?"

"The third angel was Anacapa," he beamed. "My grandfather."

The End

About the Author:

Chanel Smith is the bestselling author of 16 novels, including the The Ghost Files series, The Huntress Trilogy, and The Pack Trilogy.

Made in the USA
Las Vegas, NV
15 February 2021